A Crime of Hate

(A Detective Jackson Mystery)
L.J. Sellers

A CRIME OF HATE

Cover art by David MacFarlane
Ebook formatting by Barb Elliott

ISBN: 978-0-9987930-9-2
Published in the USA by Spellbinder Press

Cast of Characters:

Wade Jackson: detective/Violent Crimes Unit

Katie Jackson: Jackson's daughter

Kera Kollmorgan: Jackson's girlfriend/nurse

Lara Evans: detective/task force member

Rob Schakowski (Schak): detective/task force member

Michael Quince: detective/task force member

Denise Lammers: Jackson's supervisor/sergeant

Sophie Speranza: newspaper reporter

Jasmine Parker: evidence technician

Joe Berloni: evidence technician

Rich Gunderson: medical examiner/attends crime scenes

Rudolph Konrad: pathologist/performs autopsies

Pham Thi Boc: assault victim

Cam Le: murder victim

Buck Hinsic: Homelander (white nationalist) and suspect

Jola Shaffer: murder victim

Jeff Griffen: Jola's husband and suspect

Carene Zindler: Jola's sister

Lisa Priven: Jeff Griffen's sister

Chapter 1

Sunday, July 7, 10:45 p.m.

Cam Le stepped out of her room, pleased to be out of the motel. The smell had troubled her since she arrived. She couldn't even describe it, because it was so different from anything she'd known. Her peaceful home in the countryside was so different from this busy place. The last few days had been a barrage of new sights and experiences, but she was determined to follow through with her mission. Her mother's dying wish.

Cam buttoned her thin jacket against the cool night air and set off walking. After a few breaths of fresh air, she hummed a song from her childhood to soothe her anxiety. The phone in her pocket displayed a map of her route, but she didn't need to follow it. She'd memorized the way. Plus, it was safer to keep the device out of sight. She'd heard that muggers would kill for a phone, and the lateness of the hour worried her. She moved quickly, feeling both eager and nervous about the encounter. Her message would probably not be welcome, but it was critically important. For the first time in her life, she felt like she was part of something bigger than herself.

At the corner, she turned off the main street and was soon enveloped by quiet. The shortcut through the industrial area would save her time.

Ten minutes later, as she approached her destination, she

heard a car on the road behind her. Most likely, the man she'd come here to meet. Her pulse escalated and Cam braced herself. This would either be the beginning of a new life for her or the end of a long journey.

Chapter 2

Monday, July 8, 8:42 a.m.

Detective Wade Jackson stepped into the hospital room, relieved there were no visitors to deal with. He walked to the end of the bed and cleared his throat. The old man opened his eyes and sat up. The baggy hospital gown didn't hide his thin, scarred arms. Jackson glanced at his notepad and hoped he would say the guy's name correctly. "Pham Thi Boc?"

"Call me Boc." The old guy tried to smile, but his expression radiated pain.

"So Pham is your surname?"

"Yes, my family name."

Jackson circled it. That's how he and his team would refer to the victim. Pham had been assaulted the night before by a man wielding something heavy, like a pipe. Jackson usually investigated homicides, but his hometown of Eugene, Oregon was blissfully quiet for murders at the moment. His unit investigated all violent crimes though, and assaults were almost daily occurrences, so they kept busy. "Tell me what happened."

"I heard noise downstairs, behind kitchen, so I got up to see what happening." His speech was clear but a little choppy.

Jackson wondered how long he'd been in the US. "You live above the restaurant?"

"Yes. Alone now. My wife passed recently."

"I'm sorry for your loss." Jackson nodded to show his

sincerity. "You went outside?"

"Yes. I had flashlight, and I saw big man breaking windows. I yelled at him and got out phone to call police. He laughed and called me 'Chinaman.' Then I was afraid. I tried to get inside but he attacked me." The victim touched the white bandage wrapping part of his head. "Here and on shoulder." He shifted positions and grimaced.

Jackson's grip on the pen tightened. *Why would anyone hit this frail old man?* "Can you tell me anything about the attacker? How tall, for example?"

"Big. Like you. Only skinnier."

Jackson suppressed a smile and jotted down *6 ft, 190?* "What about his face?"

"I no see. He wore a stocking." Pham shook his head. "Not stocking. Like cowboy."

"A bandana?"

"Yes. I think so."

That would make the case challenging. "What about his clothes?"

The victim shrugged. "It was dark and his clothes were dark, but his arms were bare." Something sparked in the old man's dark, weary eyes. "He had a tattoo on right side." Pham rubbed his own forearm from wrist to elbow.

"Any details?"

"No. I just see ... contrast. Black ink on white arm."

Jackson wrote down *Caucasian, dark T-shirt.* "Do you know anyone who would want to attack you? Any personal grievances?" He thought he knew the answer but had to ask.

"No. I make customers happy. Family is happy. Except to lose our sweet Lam."

Just to be sure there was no connection, Jackson asked, "How did she die?"

"Cancer."

"Have you or your restaurant been targeted before?"

"Years ago, my building sprayed with paint." He struggled for a word. "Graffiti?"

That was common along the bike path and downtown where teenagers and homeless people hung out, but not in this area. Unless it was personal. "Did they find the guy?"

"No."

Jackson needed more information about the current assault but wasn't optimistic. "What time did the attack happen last night?" The police report indicated the 911 call had come in at 10:47, but he needed firsthand information. Especially if there had been a time lag. With assaults, patrol officers handled the initial response, then handed the files over to the detectives in the Violent Crimes Unit. Thank goodness. His life was chaotic enough just being called out to death scenes and campus riots.

"Ten-thirty or so. I had just gone to sleep."

"What exactly did he say?"

"He say, 'Go home, Chinaman. This is our country.'" The old man's face was stoic. "I'm Viet, not Chinese."

The perp was probably another white nationalist. They were emboldened now, and the number of bar fights and assaults the department had to deal with had doubled.

"Have you ever seen the attacker before? In or around your restaurant?"

"No. But I cook, not wait on people. And most of my customers are like me and want food from our home country. Or they old people." The guy tried to smile.

"If I find a suspect, I'll show you his photo and a close-up of his tattoo. Will you be able to identify him?"

"I don't know."

Jackson handed Pham a business card. "If you think of anything else, let me know. I'll do my best to find this guy."

The victim's expression tightened. "I buy gun for next time."

Oh boy. "Maybe install a security alarm instead."

"Too expensive. Gun is cheap."

It was the man's constitutional right, and Jackson couldn't blame him. Two other Asian restaurants had been targeted with vandalism in the last two weeks, and an import-shop owner had been pushed around. But Pham was the first to confront the perp and get hurt. The conflict and aggression had probably been stimulating to the thug and might have triggered an escalation. Other Asian shop owners could be in danger. "We'll send extra patrols by your place at night. And now that we know about his tattoo, we can probably find him."

Or not. A lot of criminals sported ink. Hell, everyone had tats now. "I'll be in touch." Jackson nodded and walked out, a mix of emotions propelling him. Anger that hate crimes were happening in his otherwise inclusive community and frustration that he didn't have a decent description. But the upside was that the perp was likely also an addict or thief and would end up in jail one way or another.

The hospital hallway seemed to close in as Jackson hurried toward the elevator. He hated the place, even though doctors here had saved his life a few times. Including last month, when he'd finally had another surgery to remove more of the fibrotic growth that was trying to kill his kidneys. He still had pain from the incision sometimes, but it was nothing compared to what he'd endured before. But the growth would come back, and he'd likely have another procedure someday—unless researchers came up with a better treatment. The prednisone he took intermittently only slowed the disease. And made him gain weight. He glanced down at his belly, thinking he should work out more—in case Kera ever wanted to get naked again.

His girlfriend was probably in the building somewhere, interviewing for a job. He hoped she instead took the nursing position at the small medical clinic down the street from his home. Kera only wanted to work part-time, so she could help care for the young boys they both had in their lives. At the moment, they were more like roommates than a couple, but he hoped that would change.

On the elevator, Jackson checked his phone for the time. Too early to head home. On the walk to his car, he called his daughter. Katie preferred text, and he indulged her sometimes, but he was a busy man. He could walk and talk. And drive and talk. But texting required stopping, getting out his reading glasses, and forcing his thick fingers to type a message without errors.

Katie picked up, sounding cheerful. Probably because she had just graduated from high school. "Hey, Dad. What's up?"

"Just checking in. Will you pick up Benjie?"

"Don't I always?"

"You often do. And I thank you."

"That it?"

"I may be late. I'm on my way to find an informant, so anything could happen."

"Stay safe."

"I'm not worried about my safety and you shouldn't be either." Jackson reached his city-issued sedan and unlocked it. "Just letting you know I might be late for dinner. Criminals and informants don't process time the same way we do."

"I know. I'll make something that will keep warm in the

oven."

"Thanks." He paid his daughter to take care of her little brother and cook meals, but he still felt guilty about it. It kept her out of trouble though, and for that he was grateful.

"Does Kera like meat? Will she be here?"

"Yes, you know she does. We've all eaten together many times. And I'm sure she'll be done interviewing by then. See you in a bit." Jackson hung up, climbed into his car, and made another call. This one went to voicemail. "Hey, TJ. It's Uncle Wade. I need your help with something. Text your location."

The sun had broken through the clouds, so Jackson took off his sports jacket, drove out of the massive parking lot, and got on the express back toward Eugene. TJ lived in the Whit, as it was now called by the hipsters who hung out there drinking locally-brewed beer. But for old-timers like himself, the fringes of the low-end neighborhood were still known as Heroin Alley. He knew where his informant lived, or had lived, but he hesitated to walk up to the guy's door. Even with just his black pullover, Jackson realized he still looked like a cop. And he didn't want to burn one of his only decent street sources.

The freeway hadn't clogged with after-work traffic yet, so he made good time. Ten minutes later, he parked in the corner of the Red Apple's parking lot, located across the street from TJ's apartment complex. As Jackson picked up his phone to call again, it buzzed. He checked the text message: *I'm home. Give me ten and I'll meet you at Prava's.*

Perfect. The meet-up might still turn out to be a waste of time, but at least he could check off this possibility. Jackson walked over to the little hole-in-the-wall restaurant, blinking in the bright sun. After three weeks of rain, he was relieved to see the sky. He stepped inside and breathed in the pleasant aroma of simmering beef and basil. The business now served Thai food, but many different chefs had come and gone over the years. So had the informants he met here.

Jackson ordered black coffee and resisted the food server's suggestion of a pastry to go with it. He still had hopes Kera would stop sleeping on the couch and come back to his bed. He was already down a few pounds and liked how it felt. But his relationship with Kera was more strained than his belt. She'd left Eugene for eight months to take care of her ailing parents, and while she was gone, he'd almost had an affair with another detective. A woman he loved as a friend . . . and possibly more. But at the time, he'd thought Kera wasn't coming back.

Nearly a half-hour later, as Jackson considered leaving, TJ finally waltzed in. Only twenty-seven, he looked a decade older, his cheeks hollow from missing most of his back teeth and his facial skin sagging from nicotine use.

"Hey. Sorry if I'm late. My girlfriend is having a rough day." TJ slid into the booth across from him, smelling like wet dog and cigarettes.

Jackson didn't ask about the girlfriend because he didn't want to know. He leaned forward. "I'm looking for a guy about my size with a tattoo on his right forearm. Probably a skinhead or white nationalist type."

"That's all you got?"

"He's been targeting Asian restaurants along West Eleventh. Last night, the perp assaulted an owner who confronted him. A frail old guy who's in the hospital and lucky to be alive."

"Targeting how?"

"Rocks through windows and some graffiti."

"Show me the tag. They all have a signature, you know."

Jackson knew. So did the property-crimes detectives who were working the vandalism cases. "Our experts don't recognize his style, so they don't think he's part of a gang." Jackson pulled out his phone and showed TJ a picture of the weird symbols the perp had spray-painted on the first two buildings.

The informant shook his dirty hair. "I've never seen anything like that. But I'll ask around and see what I can find out."

"Quickly, please, before anyone else gets hurt." Jackson put away his phone and pulled on his jacket.

"Hey, you gotta give me something for my time," TJ whined.

Jackson took a ten from his wallet and slid it across the table. "If you want real money, I need real information." He hurried out, ready to shake off the grit of the day and be home with his family.

Chapter 3

He parked in the driveway of the home he'd lived in for most of his life and sat for a moment, relishing the quiet. Kera's car was out front, so he knew she and her grandson were inside. Whenever the two boys were together, the activity and volume could be overwhelming. Raising these little men would be so different from taking care of Katie. So much more work. His daughter had matured early—most likely because her mother had been an alcoholic and she'd had to be responsible. So his daughter had needed company but not much supervision. And she'd been quiet, even with friends around. But he loved the boys and looked forward to doing guy stuff with them when they were older.

Jackson grabbed his satchel and headed inside. The sound of laughter greeted him at the door. Katie sat at the kitchen table staring at her phone. She looked up, gave him a quick wave, then went back to reading. Jackson took his weapon straight to the gun safe in his bedroom, then hurried back to the living room. Kera was on the floor with the boys, helping them build a tower with colorful Legos. Her beauty took his breath away. Classic cheekbones, perfect symmetry, and full lips. But no features that could be called delicate. Still, when she walked into a room, everyone—men and women alike—turned to stare. Tall and striking, she would always command attention..

"Daddy!" Benjie was the first to notice him. The boy ran

and leapt into his arms. Jackson hugged him tightly. Eighteen months earlier, he'd found Benjie under the house at a crime scene where his mother had been murdered, and the boy had clung to him. With no relatives to take him, social services had relented and let Benjie stay with Jackson. Now he couldn't imagine his life without this sweet child.

"Hey, my turn." Kera stepped up.

Benjie reluctantly let go, and Jackson pulled Kera in for a tight hug too. "How was your day?"

"Excellent. I got my old job back at Planned Parenthood. Half-time, as requested."

"Great news." Jackson sat on the couch, his feet aching. But he knew better than to take off his shoes. If he did, he'd get called back to work. Kera sat next to him, and her grandson came up to Jackson and hugged his legs. The boy had been bonded to him, but Kera had taken Micah and been gone for eight months. In the perspective of a five-year-old, that was eternity, so they were sort of starting over. "Hey, Micah. How was your day?"

"I went to school. With Benj. We practiced colors."

"What's your favorite?"

"Blue, like the water."

Jackson smiled. "Me too." He'd once owned and restored a midnight-blue 1968 GTO. But he'd sold it to pay for his daughter's therapy after her mother died. Both thoughts made his heart ache for what could have been.

Katie came into the living room and announced dinner was ready. They all moved into the kitchen, and Jackson gave his daughter a quick one-armed hug. That was all he could get away with. But she smiled sincerely. She'd been happy and pleasant lately. And suddenly that worried him.

Four bites into his meal, his phone rang. Jackson's gut

tightened as he checked the ID. *Lammers.* He stepped away from the table as he took the call. "Jackson here. What have you got?"

"A homicide. A transient found her body near a dumpster."

"Where?" Jackson hurried to retrieve his weapon and jacket. As he walked away, he heard Katie mumble about him getting a new case.

"Behind the Golden Dragon restaurant," Lammers said. "Apparently it's closed on Mondays so we don't know how long the corpse has been there."

"That's on West Eleventh, correct?"

"Yes. Not far from the last assault case I assigned you."

"Oh crap. We have to get more patrols out in that area until we find this guy. If it's the same perp."

"I'll call your usual team, but we are understaffed." She let out a frustrated grunt. "And we're taking a PR hit on these assaults already."

"I'm on my way."

Jackson stepped into the kitchen and apologized to his family, then kissed Benjie's forehead. "I'll say goodnight when I get home, even if you're sleeping."

"Bye, Daddy. Be safe."

Kera stood. "I'll walk you out."

When they were outside, she said, "I looked at a couple of houses today. One rental and one for sale."

His heart sank, even though he'd known this day was coming. "I'll miss you. I'm sorry I don't have more space here." She'd been sleeping on his couch and living out of suitcases since she got back. His emergency surgery had thrown both their lives off-kilter for a while.

"I'm looking at big places. For all of us." Kera gave him a soft smile. "We might as well keep being roommates and parents to each other's children."

Jackson beamed, not even trying to hide his relief. He needed her in so many ways. "Great idea." They'd been looking at rentals together before her mother got sick. "What area?"

"This neighborhood. I know you like it here."

Jackson leaned in and kissed her cheek. "I love you." He turned and strode to his car, not wanting to put her on the spot. But he was holding onto the idea that she still loved him—and would forgive him someday.

Chapter 4

Staring into the setting sun, he raced out West Eleventh, more out of habit than necessity. Or maybe it was the adrenaline. He loved the challenge of solving homicides, and the first few hours of a new case were strangely exhilarating. He'd never told anyone that—except Evans, because he knew she felt the same way. The only bad moment at a crime scene was staring at the body and trying to visualize the victim's last few minutes of life. Autopsies, which came later, could be challenging too, especially with dead women. He hoped the victim wasn't young or female.

Flashing red and blue lights ahead signaled the location, and Jackson slowed to make the turn. He parked behind a patrol unit and gathered his crime-scene tools. His satchel held most of what he needed, but the box of latex gloves was on the floor in the back, and his flashlight was under the front seat. He would need it soon when the sun went down. A moment he dreaded. Crime-scene analysis outside and in the dark tended to make him feel incompetent. His adrenaline rush fading a bit, he climbed out.

Jackson glanced at the restaurant, recalling that he'd eaten there once long ago. A curved front facade had been added to an otherwise no-nonsense structure, and the words *Golden Dragon* flashed in yellow neon above the door. The windows were dark, and the lack of light was an invitation for crime. In the small front parking lot, the medical examiner's van hadn't arrived yet, but Jackson spotted another blue sedan like his own. Evans, he guessed. She often was the first team member to arrive.

Jackson nodded at the patrol officer standing watch and headed to the back. Another patrol officer was stringing crime-scene tape between the dumpster and the back of the building, and a body lay on the ground about five feet from the base of the trash container. At least the poor woman hadn't been tossed inside like an earlier victim. The case that had brought Kera into his life.

Evans kneeled next to the body but wasn't touching it. She was only five-five, but her strength and athleticism still amazed him.

Jackson walked up and stood next to her. "What have we got?"

"Bludgeoned female with no ID. But I called the owners, and they're coming down to see if she's an employee." Her heart-shaped face always made him smile. Perps who mistook her for a softie often got their asses kicked.

Jackson squatted, grimacing at the pain in his still-healing incision. With a gloved hand, he lifted the dead woman's arm. Even through the latex, he could tell she was cold and stiff. *Damn.* The perp had a long head start already. Jackson aimed his flashlight on the dead woman's face, and the eerie image of her blood-soaked head seared into his brain. But she was obviously Asian. "Head trauma like our last victim."

"Multiple blows," Evans said, her voice tight. "She didn't go down easy."

They were both quiet for a moment, and Jackson cursed the looming darkness. If there were footprints or dropped cigarette butts, he couldn't see them. The crime-scene techs would arrive soon with bright work lights and begin an inch-by-inch search. But for the moment, his team had nothing to go on—except the victim's appearance. "She looks thirty or so."

"Older, I think," Evans countered. "Look at her clothes."

Jackson ran the light slowly along her body. A petite woman, wearing baggy cotton garments and flip-flops. "What was she doing back here?"

"She doesn't look homeless and the restaurant is closed, so she probably wasn't working today." Evans turned to him. "Maybe she lives around here."

Jackson didn't even bother to look up. The main thoroughfare was lined with restaurants, auto stores, and paint suppliers. And behind them was an industrial area. "There is no housing here. Unless she walked over from City View or that next connector on the west side."

"You mean Oak Patch?" Evans grinned at him. "Senior moment?"

"I hope not." Jackson longed for a cup of coffee to recharge his tired brain and body. "But I take that back about no housing. Pham, the victim I talked to in the hospital today, said he lived above his restaurant. So there might be a few apartments scattered around." He glanced at the single-story Golden Dragon. "But I don't see any square footage for living space in there."

Jackson pushed up the victim's sleeves, looking for self-defense wounds—and didn't see any. "Where's the transient who found her body?"

"We don't know." Evans stood to stretch. "He apparently flagged down a patrol car, yelled something about a body, then disappeared while the officer was turning around."

Bracing himself, Jackson scooted closer to the woman's head and aimed his flashlight at her wounds. The blood had dried long ago, but it had flowed from two distinct gashes about four inches apart. She'd been struck twice by a blunt, heavy object. An image of a big man, wielding a lead pipe or a long flashlight like his, popped into his mind. He visualized the thug chasing the tiny woman across the parking lot, then striking her from behind. Or maybe he'd walked up to her, hiding his weapon and pretending to need help. Or jumped out from behind the dumpster.

All the scenarios sickened him. "If the same perp who assaulted Pham also attacked this victim, then we're looking for someone my size with a tattoo on his forearm."

"Well, that narrows it down to about a hundred suspects."

"He's also a white nationalist, or at least someone who hates Asians." *Or just their restaurants?*

"Okay, fifty suspects." Evans let out a soft laugh.

Jackson got up, his knees aching. A clatter of footsteps made him turn. Rich Gunderson, the medical examiner, and his team had arrived. Carrying a heavy set of work lights, Gunderson sounded breathless when he barked, "Get away from the body!"

Jackson and Evans stepped back, and a team of headlamp-wearing crime-scene techs started combing the area. Gunderson, wearing his usual black-on-black, was nearly invisible. "What do we know?" he asked, squatting near the victim.

"Almost nothing." Worry dropped like a rock in Jackson's stomach. The woman had no ID and had been dead for a while, so their chance of bringing her justice seemed slim. "We have no idea who she is, but we think she's been dead since last night or early this morning."

Gunderson gave him a look. "Time of death is my job. I'll get her temp and let you know. Go look for witnesses or something and let me work."

"If you find any significant body markers, I want to know immediately. We have to identify her."

"That, on the other hand, is your job." Gunderson chuckled. "She's not likely to have a tramp stamp with her name."

Jackson bit back a response and jogged back around to the front of the building.

Evans stayed right with him. "Did you learn anything from the assault vic at the hospital? Any obvious connections?"

"Just the partial description I mentioned of the perp's size and forearm tattoo." Another detail surfaced. "He also mentioned that the assailant specifically said, 'Go home, Chinaman.'"

"Does that tell us anything about the perp?" Evans stopped. "Would a young person use that expression?"

"I think it's universal to anyone who's ethnocentric. People who see Americans, or Caucasians, as superior tend to think all Asians are the same. The old guy is Vietnamese, by the way."

"You know that expression is inappropriate?" A smile played on Evans' face. "They're just Viet. The way we're Americans, not Americanese."

"Huh." Jackson had never thought about it. "How do you know this?"

"I read." Evans started walking again. "You should try it."

In the front parking lot, they approached two patrol officers. As the men turned, Jackson asked, "Has anyone canvassed the area?"

"I just got back," the younger officer said. He looked twenty. Jackson didn't know either one. The department had hired dozens of new recruits in the last year.

Jackson suddenly felt old. "Anything?"

"The businesses around here are all closed, and I only encountered one pedestrian. I checked his ID and got his name and number, but he's fifty-two and has no criminal record."

"What's his size?" Everyone was a suspect . . . until they weren't.

"Five-nine and slender. Dressed well too, so not homeless. He said he was meeting someone for a drink and didn't want to be late."

"Send me his name and information." It would likely end up as only a note in his file. Jackson wasn't optimistic about solving this one. His only real hope was that the restaurant had security cameras. But even if they did, the crime had likely occurred out of their reach.

The other officer spoke up. "I talked with a guy on a bike when I first got here. He looked thirty-five and was your size."

Jackson's interest perked up. "And?"

"He said his name was Travis Grabski, but he didn't have any proof of that. He claimed he was on his way to work at a bakery downtown."

"You doubt that?"

The officer shrugged. "The work part, yes. He's probably a druggie on his way to his dealer."

"How was he dressed? Any tattoos?"

"No ink that I could see. Wearing jeans and a heavy coat. Dark hair and eyes and a goatee."

The heavy coat didn't match what Pham had said about the perp. Still, Jackson was irritated. "You didn't detain him?"

The officer stiffened. "I watched him ride up the street, like he was just passing by. He wasn't anywhere near the back of the building."

"Okay. Write up the report and send it to me." Jackson resisted the urge to sigh. Without the victim's name they couldn't even notify her family, let alone question associates. Business owners in the area might know her, but they were not likely available at this point in the evening. Still, he had to try.

A car pulled in and the group turned. It was another dark Impala. A burly older man climbed out and hurried over with surprising speed. Rob Schakowski had buzzed his hair so tight, the sweat on his scalp glimmered in the building's neon light. "Hey, sorry I'm late. I had to jumpstart this piece of shit."

The young patrol officer chuckled. "You need one of these new SUVs. Comfy and dependable."

That would never happen. Another way his unit got shortchanged. Jackson turned to Schak. "We've got a dead woman, probably in her thirties, and no ID."

"Stiff body and no witnesses either," Evans added. "And Gunderson says she wasn't dumped here either."

"Oh good. An easy one." Schak rolled his eyes.

Jackson leaned in to see if he could smell alcohol. His partner and friend had started self-medicating on the job after Schak's cousin, another officer, had died. Jackson had finally had to speak to him about it, but now Schak seemed to have quit drinking entirely . . . again.

"What's my assignment?" Schak met his eyes.

"Mugshots and patrol reports," Jackson said. "We're looking for a guy about my size with a tattoo on his right forearm. And a bad attitude toward Asian people." Was the word *Asian* still politically correct? he wondered.

"Will do. Maybe if my car breaks down in the department parking lot, they'll finally issue me a new one." Schak nodded and turned toward his sedan. "If anything goes down, call me."

Before Jackson could assign further tasks, another vehicle pulled in. The oversized SUV stopped short, blocking the entrance.

"I hope these are the owners." Evans shifted on her feet.

An older couple climbed out, both tall and slender . . . and Caucasian. That surprised him. He stepped toward them. "Detective Jackson, Eugene Police."

The man held out his hand. "George and Alice Moreland. We own this restaurant."

Jackson shook his hand, then the woman spoke up. "We only bought it a year ago. The lovely Cambodian couple who owned it for decades finally retired."

Evans cut in, introducing herself. "I'm the one who called you. Are you ready to look at the body?"

The older woman nodded. "Let's get this over with." She walked off with Evans while her husband stayed put, surprising Jackson again.

"How can I help?" the owner asked.

"Just answer a few questions, please." Jackson decided to ask the important one first. This man didn't look like he had anything to hide. "Where were you last night and early this morning?" He hoped Evans would come back with not just an ID but a time of death too.

Moreland blinked and rocked back. "You suspect me?"

"We suspect everyone until we know for sure." Jackson pulled out his notepad.

"I was home in bed. With my wife. As always. We got up around seven this morning."

Jackson would let that go unless the evidence started to point back at the owners. "What about the restaurant? Anything unusual happen here lately?"

"Someone tagged the building a few months ago, but the security camera caught him. He was arrested, and nothing has happened since." Moreland's voice was articulate but aging.

Jackson stared at the man's face, but in the dark, it was hard to guess his age. "What's the man's name?"

"Brett Wright, age 21. He's still in jail. When they arrested him, he assaulted an officer."

A dead end for the homicide investigation. "What made you decide to buy this restaurant?"

"We're both retired teachers. We got bored and started taking cooking classes. Then Alice decided she needed a bigger kitchen." Moreland chuckled. "So we bought this one."

Rapid footsteps sounded behind him. Jackson turned to see Evans coming back, with Alice Moreland right behind her. The woman headed straight for her SUV and climbed in.

Evans looked at Jackson and shook her head. "The victim isn't an employee or anyone they know."

Crap. "What about time of death? Did Gunderson give you anything?"

"Around midnight last night, give or take an hour in either direction."

Dread filled his stomach. They had missed their window of opportunity to find the killer before he destroyed evidence, left town, and/or established an alibi. A darker thought hit him. The perp, if they were dealing with the same guy, had escalated his attacks. The first had occurred two weeks earlier—a woman pushed around and verbally abused as she left her Asian-import store late at night. But now the old man in the hospital and the Jane Doe by the dumpster had been violently assaulted within an hour of each other. Maybe their perp had been high on meth or PCP and had gone on a rampage the night before. But whatever had triggered him, he was likely to strike again. And possibly soon.

"What are you thinking?" Evans asked.

"That our perp is escalating and we don't have time to waste."

"Let's get the victim's photo out to the public now. I'll contact broadcasters and push for coverage on the late news tonight. But it's probably too late for that. So maybe we can get the image into the morning's newspaper."

"As much as it pains me, I'll call Sophie Speranza and ask for her help." The reporter was irritating and pushy but also resourceful and tenacious. Jackson had come to respect her, but he still hated talking to her.

Evans elbowed him. "You know you like her now."

Jackson made a face, then turned to the patrol cops. "Get a photo of the victim and start showing it around the apartments over on Oak Patch and City View. We need an ID."

"Yes, sir." The officers hustled off.

Jackson was tempted to check in with the ME again, but Gunderson would already be annoyed by the patrol cops taking photos, so he decided to skip it. Evans had gone to her car to make calls so he did the same.

On the third ring, the reporter's face was suddenly on his phone. "Hey, Jackson. You made a FaceTime call. This must be important."

FaceTime? Ugh. "I didn't mean to open the video, but this will be quick. We need to get a victim's photo in the paper in the morning so we can identify her. "

"Another corpse? My editor hates those."

"Please make it happen. Two people were assaulted Sunday night and one is dead. We need to ID this victim and find her killer before anyone else is hurt."

"Let me grab my notepad."

As she stepped away, Jackson caught movement in the background of the video image. Someone was going out Sophie's front door. Tall and thin with long black hair. Was that Jasmine Parker—his favorite crime-scene tech?

Chapter 5

A few minutes earlier

Sophie Speranza sashayed up to her girlfriend and pulled her in for a seductive hug. "I missed you."

"I was only gone four days," Jasmine whispered with her mouth pressed against Sophie's.

A phone beeped like an alarm from somewhere in the room. Jasmine pulled back. "That's my boss."

"Just ignore it. Please." Sophie knew she was wasting her breath.

"I can't. You know that." Jasmine searched her purse for the cell. "You wouldn't ignore a call from work either. What we both do is too important." Jasmine finally located her phone on the couch and took the call. "It's Parker. What's happening?"

Sophie watched her intently, wishing she would put the phone on speaker.

"Sorry," Jasmine said to her boss, while giving Sophie a look. "I was in the shower and must have missed your first call." After a pause, she said, "On my way," and hung up. Jasmine pulled on her sweater and turned to Sophie. "A new homicide scene and I'm already late. Did you hear my phone earlier?"

"No, I was in the kitchen." Sophie resisted the urge to grab her own sweater. She would follow her girlfriend to the crime scene, but Jasmine didn't need to know that. A moment later, her own phone rang, surprising her. Sophie grabbed it from the coffee table. *Detective Jackson.* What was going on? "It's Jackson," she said, noticing Jasmine had paused.

Sophie answered the call, and his face appeared on her screen. *What the hell?* "Hey, Jackson. You made a FaceTime call. This must be important."

The detective grunted. "I didn't mean to open the video, but this will be quick. We need to get a victim's photo in the paper in the morning so we can identify her."

"Another corpse? My editor hates those." But her supervisor was home and drunk by now, so she wouldn't even ask him.

"Just make it happen," Jackson said in his usual stern voice. "Two people were assaulted Sunday night and one is dead. We need to ID the second one and find her killer before anyone else is hurt."

"Let me grab my notepad." Sophie scooted to her desk and waved at Jasmine as her still-in-the-closet girlfriend headed out. She grabbed a yellow tablet, put on her earpiece, and asked, "What two victims?"

She heard Jackson sigh. "The first was Pham Boc, who was defending his restaurant from a vandal. He's in the hospital. But the second victim died from similar wounds. She wasn't found until this evening."

Whoa. That was quite an info dump. "Please text me the spelling on that name. Then tell me which restaurant." Sophie scribbled notes as fast as she could, hoping Jackson would take a moment to send the text and let her catch up.

"Lucky Noodle on Garfield."

She knew the place. "Did he identify his attacker?"

"He gave a general description. Six feet, one-ninety or so, and a tattoo on his forearm."

"I can use that, correct? It might generate some leads."

"Yes, but I need to wrap this up and get back to work."

"Where was the second victim found?"

"Behind the Golden Dragon restaurant on West Eleventh."

A definite pattern was emerging. "Is the dead woman Asian too? These sound like hate crimes." She remembered the vandalism incidents from a few weeks ago. They could all be connected.

"We don't know," Jackson said, sounding frustrated. "Just tell me where to send her image. It's on my phone."

"Text it to this number and I'll take it from there."

"Thanks." Jackson disconnected before she could ask more questions. But her phone pinged a moment later. While she checked the text for the male victim's spelling, a second message came in with an image attached. *Ugh.* Poor woman. She hoped they caught the bastard.

Sophie grabbed her sweater and matching red purse and charged out the door. She would swing by the crime scene and grab a photo of the activity—or at least a silhouette of the red and blue flashing lights in the darkness—if she could get close enough. Then she would drive out to the *Willamette News* building. She could probably accomplish her task over the phone, but the night editors hated redoing layout at the last minute and it would be harder for them to say no to her face. And, if she wanted the victim's photo on the website, she would have to upload it herself. After finally selling out to a media conglomerate, the paper had laid off so many more people she was now her own photographer and web editor too. She went to work every day expecting it to be her last.

As she trotted downstairs, the roar of the river greeted her. A thrilling sound for someone who'd grown up in dry Arizona. Which was why she'd chosen this building. These were the only apartments on the affordable side of the river.

The night traffic was minimal, and the drive across town took only a few minutes. She loved that about Eugene too. Just big enough to host a couple of colleges and a handful of performance theaters but small enough geographically that everything seemed accessible. Sophie spotted the patrol lights ahead and slowed, looking for a place to park nearby. She pulled into the auto-parts store adjacent to the Golden Dragon, adjusted the settings on her camera, and hopped out. As a patrol officer barreled toward her, Sophie quickly took as many images as she could.

"Hey, put that camera down! What are you doing here?" The cop's hand was on his weapon.

"Sophie Speranza, *Willamette News*." She tossed the camera into her car and clicked her fob to lock it. "I'm on assignment. In fact, I'm on my way to the newspaper now to get the victim's image into the morning paper—as requested by Detective Jackson."

"Huh. Well then, get moving."

Sophie smiled, jumped back into her car, and waved as she drove out.

Another fifteen minutes and she arrived at the oversized building with a massive parking lot in back. Three cars were parked near the main entrance while four more sat behind the three-story printing-press structure. The new owners published a variety of advertising supplements, and many were printed here and shipped out. It kept the money flowing . . . for the moment. Everyone in the building knew their days were numbered, including her. She'd been building a freelance career as a political-news blogger and had started writing a novel as her next career. Before meeting Jasmine, she'd planned to move to a bigger city, likely Portland, but now she hoped to make it work here in Eugene when they finally laid her off.

Inside, she sat at her desk and booted up her computer. After transferring her photo files, she resized the dead woman's image and loaded it onto the server, then sent the night editor an email. She should have called him but didn't want to get yelled at.

Her cell phone rang a few minutes later. Sophie reluctantly picked up. "Hey."

"This is bullshit, you know. I just finished the final layout."

"I know. I'm sorry. But we're helping the police. This poor woman has people who care about her and need to know what happened."

"I get that. But I don't really care about this job anymore and I'm leaving work on time, no matter how crappy the city page looks."

"As long as you get this image printed, we're good."

The old man snorted and hung up.

Sophie opened the website-editing software and uploaded the photo onto their home page. She added a caption and two phone numbers, hers and Jackson's. She hoped whoever responded would call her first. Her crime stories were usually the most read pieces in the paper, and tracking down the important details kept her employed.

Before wrapping up, she called Jasmine, hoping for a crime-scene scoop, but her girlfriend didn't respond. She would see her later and find out everything Jasmine could safely tell her. No one in the police department knew about their relationship, and Jasmine wanted to keep it that way. Sophie wished they could be out in the open, but she also loved getting inside information. That would likely stop if Jackson or the ME knew they were dating. Jasmine wouldn't take the risk.

Sophie closed down her files and headed back out, adrenaline still flowing. Maybe she would stop by the crime scene again. Working odd hours suited her. She hoped to never be the kind of person who sat at home every night watching TV. Sophie tried to visualize herself as an old woman and laughed out loud. She was still smiling when she reached her car.

Chapter 6

Lara Evans was too wound up to call it a night. There had to be something productive she could accomplish. Their victim had already been dead for nearly twenty-four hours, and they had no idea who she was. The one thing they knew was that the murder was likely a hate crime. On impulse, she called Carla River, an FBI agent they'd worked with on other cases, who was now assigned to domestic terrorists and hate groups.

After five rings, River finally answered. "Hey, Evans. I assume this is important."

"Yes. Sorry to bother you so late." Evans started her car to get some heat going. The night air was cooling off quickly. "We have a homicide, an Asian woman with no ID. We think it's a hate crime."

"I'm sorry to hear that. I saw the vandalism reports from a few weeks ago, but I haven't had a chance to follow up. I've been working with a task force in Portland."

"Are you focused on a particular group?"

"The Homelanders. In Portland they've been targeting mostly Hispanic laborers. But they also go after Asian business owners who don't employ any white people." River made a noise in her throat. "Whatever *white* means anymore."

"I won't even respond to the hypocrisy. But tell me more. Sometimes Portland gangs send people here."

"They have a subgroup in Eugene, but it's small. Hang on

a sec." For a moment there was only background noise—a door closing and soft footsteps, then River was back. "The local leader is a guy named Buck Hinsic." River spelled it out. "It's a Slavic name. And we've identified eleven of his followers because they were arrested after clashing with liberal protestors."

"Any with a forearm tattoo? Someone about six-feet tall?

"Can you give me a minute to search? I'll call you back."

"Thanks."

Evans pulled into the street. Instinctively, she headed for the Brewster, a biker bar about ten blocks away. People tended to stick to certain neighborhoods—to shop, socialize, search for drugs, and, for some people, to patrol as their home turf.

As Evans pulled into the tavern side lot, River called back. "I've got a name for you. Ray Frost. He's thirty-two, lives in Eugene, and works as a mechanic. Or he did. I'll text you his last known address."

"Thanks. Send me a photo too."

"Already did. And a close-up of the tattoo." River paused and shuffled some paper. "By the way, the Portland Police Bureau has an arrest warrant for him on a failure to appear in court. But the original charges are vandalism and resisting arrest, both from a demonstration clash three months ago."

"No assault?"

A pause. "He had assault charges but they were dropped."

"A solid lead. Thanks." But none of those charges would inspire police to actively search for him or allow the county jail to hold him for long. Evans clicked off and waited for the images to land in her phone. The mugshot made her slump. Buzzed head, goatee, stern expression—Frost looked like a hundred other criminals. Picking him out of a crowd would be challenging. He also looked heavier than the one-ninety the first victim had described. But a couple months of heavy drug use could make forty pounds disappear.

The tattoo image was more promising, a distinctive design of green and black geometric patterns—that looked Asian. More irony. Evans checked her weapon before getting out. Her pale-blue blazer didn't signal that she was law enforcement, but the Glock bulge was hard to hide. Three steps from her vehicle, she turned back and retrieved a stun gun from under her seat. Frost had a history of resisting arrest, and he would probably be stupid enough to underestimate her. She had trained for the SWAT-unit test by carrying a roll of carpet around her backyard, and she practiced Brazilian jiu-jitsu just for fun.

Still, she hesitated, then called Jackson. He picked up immediately.

"What have you got?"

"I'm going into the Brewster on Garfield to look for a suspect. I have no specific reason to think he's here, except proximity, but if you're still in the neighborhood, I might need backup."

"I'm talking to a possible witness. Give me ten minutes."

"Thanks." Evans disconnected before he could instruct her to wait for him. She might as well go in and start the search. This was a long shot and she regretted calling Jackson. Spending time alone with him wasn't in her best interest. She was finally dating again, and she had to give Todd and her new relationship a chance.

Inside the ugly building the noise slammed her like a physical force. A three-man band played on a corner stage, and they tried to make up for talent with volume. Cue balls clicking and men shouting to be heard added to the cacophony. Evans did her best to tune it out. She made her way past a group of tables toward the bar, quickly scanning faces and forearms. At least half the patrons were women, which surprised her. Perhaps it was Ladies' Night. But no Ray Frost.

Evans moved casually toward the pool room, resisting the beat of the music. Bad as it was, it still made her want to dance. The crowd in the side room was almost all male, and a guy leaning against the back wall, drinking a bottled beer, caught her eye. Just over six-feet with a stubble of dark hair and a ratty goatee—with tattoos on both forearms. Several men turned to watch her and Evans smiled, trying to look friendly. She stopped near the racks that held pool sticks, selected one, and pulled it out.

She expected to abandon it moments later, but she needed the prop to get close enough to her suspect to examine his face and tat design without spooking him.

"Hey, pretty lady," an older man called to her as she passed him. Evans glanced over, nodded, and kept moving past the pool tables. She wished she had a quarter to put down for a challenge game. She walked to the back wall and leaned against it, about five feet from the guy she now believed to be Ray Frost. His face was leaner than in his mugshot, making his jaws seem narrow. That and his wide-set eyes gave him a slight alien look.

Evans eased toward him, glancing at his tattoo in short intervals. A match to the mugshot.

Frost abruptly walked away. None of the men playing pool seemed to notice. Relieved, Evans left her cue stick and followed. Confronting him outside and alone was better all around. Without looking back, Frost picked up his pace as he skirted through the cocktail tables and dodged around a group standing by the door.

Evans ran after him, bumping into a cocktail waitress.

"Hey!"

She ignored the woman and tried to close the gap. Frost pushed through the door and bolted into the parking lot. Evans sprinted after him. "Stop! Eugene Police! I just want to talk."

The suspect didn't even slow down.

Evans pounded after him, pulling the taser as she ran. "Stop! Police!"

A car pulled into the lot at the far end, blocking the exit. Frost spun around and ran straight at her—like a deranged football player.

Shit! Evans jumped sideways, just clearing his path, then steadied herself. She aimed the taser for the middle of his back and fired. One prong landed in his shoulder and the other in his butt cheek. The man's glute seized up and he buckled, landing on his knees. Evans charged over to him, pulling her cuffs with her free hand.

A moment later, as she kneeled on the suspect's back to secure his wrists, a familiar voice cut through the night. "Looks like you got this under control."

Evans glanced up to see Jackson with his weapon at his side.

"Nice timing." She would have caught and cuffed the guy even without Jackson's vehicular support, but the less effort the better. This would now be a long night.

Chapter 7

At the department, Evans escorted Frost into one of the interrogation rooms—a dark, dismal space the size of a closet. She would move the suspect's handcuffs from the back to the front—after Jackson showed up. With a strong push to his shoulder, she urged Frost into the chair on the far side of the table. "I'll return with some water in a moment." Keeping an eye on him, she took two steps back before moving toward the exit.

"I'd rather have a beer!" Frost spoke for the first time. He'd been silent on the ride down, but apparently the windowless room had unnerved him a little. Evans ignored his comment and headed for the break room.

She found Jackson there, pouring a cup of crappy coffee. "Don't drink it," Evans warned. "The only thing worse than freeze-dried chemicals is burnt freeze-dried chemicals." She craved a cup of good java but nothing was open at this hour.

"You're right." Jackson poured it out.

Evans filled three paper cups with water and handed him one. "Try this stuff. It's kind of bland but your body will like it." She winked, then wished she hadn't. But flirting with him was a habit.

Jackson made a face. "Let's get a quick confession and go home for the night so I don't regret passing on the caffeine."

"I think you're dreaming, but we'll see." She started for the door. "Let me be bad cop this time. He already hates me for taking him down with a taser."

"I'll work on my fake empathy."

"And let's open with the assault on the old guy. See if he'll cop to that. Then we hit him with the murder charge."

Jackson smiled. "Good plan. Who did you learn that from?"

Evans grinned back, then pounded down the stairs to the basement.

At the entrance, she activated the video camera, just in case they got a confession. When they entered the claustrophobic room, their suspect was leaning back in his chair, eyes closed. He snapped to attention and focused on Jackson. "What is this about? You can't detain me without a reason."

Evans put a cup of water in front of Frost and gave him a shitty smile. "Too bad you're still cuffed."

"This is causing me pain, by the way." He tried to sound tough, but it came out whiny.

Evans sat down but Jackson remained standing. "I can move the cuffs to the front, but only if you cooperate."

"With what? I don't know what you want."

"The truth." Jackson stepped toward Frost. "And keep in mind that we already know the answers to most of our questions."

A bold lie. Evans held back a smile. While Jackson made the suspect more comfortable, she stated everyone's name for the camera and told the tattooed man they were recording. Then she jumped right in with an easy question to clear out the crap. "Why did you run?"

"Look, I know I missed a court date in Portland. But it's a bullshit charge from a protest I attended. I have a right to protest."

"Now you've added another resisting-arrest charge to

your file."

He hung his head for a second, then looked up with pleading eyes. "I have to work tomorrow. I can't afford to lose my job."

"You have bigger things to worry about now." Evans paused to let him sweat that for a moment, then piled on with another pressure-filled false claim. "We have footage of you near the restaurant where Mr. Pham was attacked."

"No fucking idea who you're talking about."

"The old Asian guy you assaulted," Evans said. "He described your left forearm tattoo, then we found you in the mug books, and now here we are."

Frost glanced at his arm, his eyes wide. "This is a common design."

"Not really." Evans shook her head. "He also identified your mugshot as the guy who attacked him."

"Bullshit. I always wear—" Frost stopped short.

Snap! He had just stepped halfway in. Evans struggled to repress a smile. Some criminals were pathetically stupid. "Yes, you were wearing a bandana at the time of the assault. We know. And so will the jurors who watch this video. A confession could help reduce your sentence."

"No. I didn't say that or mean that. It wasn't me. I didn't hurt that guy."

Jackson cut in, playing his part. "We know you didn't mean too. Tell us your side of the story. Mr. Pham said he caught you tagging his building."

Frost shook his head. "No. I may have tagged some property in my younger days but not anymore." He tried to sound earnest. "And I used to wear a bandana when I was a tagger. That's all I meant."

"We don't care about the graffiti," Evans said dryly. "It's

the assault we're interested in. Where were you last night?" First, they had to trap him in a lie.

"Uh, with a friend, watching TV."

"What's his or her name?"

"Ryan. I don't know his last name."

"It's not an alibi if we can't check it." Evans leaned forward. "What's his address?"

"I don't know. The house is on Fourth Street, I think. It was dark when we got there."

"Can you take us there to talk to Ryan?"

Frost's eyes went wide. "I barely know the guy. He's a friend of a friend and was letting me crash on his couch."

He clearly didn't have an alibi. "Why not just go home?"

"I'd had a lot to drink."

Time to shake him up. Evans pulled out her phone, found the photo of the murder victim, and showed it to their suspect. "What's her name?"

A flash of panic on his face. "How should I know?"

"You killed her. Are you saying she's a stranger? Someone you just attacked at random?"

"Whoa! This is crazy. I didn't kill anyone." Frost's voice kept cutting out, and he finally grabbed the water with his cuffed hands and gulped some.

"You belong to a white-nationalist hate group that targets Asian-owned businesses. You half-admitted to assaulting an old man. And you have no alibi for the evening. A night during which two Asian people were brutally attacked and one of them died." Evans shook her head. "You're going down for this."

Jackson shifted in his seat and spoke softly. "Confessing and showing remorse for her death will work in your favor."

"No. No. No." Frost shook his head with the intensity of a

wet dog. "I do have an alibi. I just can't tell you about it."

Evans laughed. "You mean you were busy committing another crime?"

Silence.

Evans leaned in. "The murder was up close and personal, and I'm sure the pathologist will find your DNA on the victim somewhere."

Frost blinked rapidly, started to speak, then stopped.

"We need to know who the victim is," Jackson added. "So we can contact her family. You owe them that. So tell us. Who is she and how do you know her?"

"I don't know her, I swear! I didn't kill her. And I have nothing more to say."

"You will sit in jail until this is resolved one way or another," Evans warned. Another fabrication. Without any serious charges, he would be promptly released. And they didn't have enough grounds to ask the district attorney to charge him yet.

Frost blinked again. And squirmed.

They waited him out.

Finally he blurted, "What if I know who might have done it?"

Chapter 8

Tuesday, July 9, 3:27 a.m.

Jackson woke to the sound of crying and bolted out of bed. He rushed to Benjie's room to comfort the boy. The damn nightmares were back, and nothing seemed to help. As he cradled his still-half-asleep son, Kera came in. Jackson suppressed a flash of anger. Kera's leaving had been traumatic for Benjie—another episode of abandonment. But Kera's mother had been sick and dying, and she'd had no choice. Sometimes life was a shit sandwich, and you couldn't help one person without hurting another.

"I can hold him," Kera said. "You need to get some sleep." She rubbed Jackson's back as she talked.

Love swelled in his heart. She was such a good woman. "Let's see how long this takes. What time is it? I might just stay up."

"It's three-thirty, and you've only been in bed for a couple hours." Kera eased the crying boy out of his arms. "Go get some sleep."

Relieved, Jackson kissed Benjie's forehead and plodded back into the bedroom. As he was drifting off, he felt Kera slide into bed. At first her presence startled him. Then he heard the boy's soft whimpers and realized his sweet girlfriend was trying to make Benjie happy. Still, she was in his bed. Jackson reached over and squeezed her hand before giving into the shutdown time he so desperately needed.

He woke an hour and a half later, slipped out of bed, and shut off the alarm before it could ring. Dressing quietly in the darkened room, he fumbled for his shoes, then retrieved his service weapon from the safe. Before stepping out, Jackson glanced at Kera one more time. He loved seeing her in his bed and hoped she never slept anywhere else. But life was so unpredictable he'd learned not to count on anything.

He checked his phone for messages and hurried out, planning to buy coffee on the way. His morning task list included stopping by the hospital to see Pham and show him two mugshots, then check the motels in the area of the murder scene—all before the task force meeting at nine. Patrol officers hadn't located a nearby car that could belong to the victim, she didn't work at the restaurant, and her body hadn't been transported from another crime scene. So he had to assume she'd arrived by foot. He had intended to check motels in the area the night before, but then Evans had found Ray Frost and they'd interrogated him instead.

Jackson pulled into a Dutch Brothers kiosk and ordered a small cup of Italian roast. He needed more caffeine than that, but the bottom half of a tall cup would get too cold to drink. While he waited, he thought about the name Frost had given them. According to what Evans had learned from the FBI, Buck Hinsic was the local leader of a white nationalist group. They'd put out an attempt-to-locate for him, booked Frost into jail for resisting arrest, then called it a night. Checking Hinsic's last known address was on Jackson's list too, but it would be a waste of time. Patrol officers would have better luck in their daily encounters with the riffraff. His team needed to find the woman's name. Her family, if she had one, deserved to know what had happened. Jackson made a mental note to check with the missing-persons detective, then paid for his coffee and started his workday.

When he walked into the hospital room, a woman in pink scrubs was leaving, and the old man was eating breakfast. Pham looked up and smiled. "Mr. Jackson. You're here so early."

"I'm sorry, but I need your help with something, and I have a task force meeting in a few hours."

"Good you are here now. I go home soon."

"Great news." Jackson reached for his phone and opened the department's database. "I need you to look at some photos and tell me if you recognize anyone."

"You found the man who attacked me?"

"We hope so." Jackson keyed in Frost's name, waited for the file to load, and showed Pham the image, even though it was a mugshot from several years earlier.

The old man reached for a pair of glasses, then squinted at the picture. "No. I never see him." He looked up at Jackson, frustrated. "I'm sorry but his face was covered."

"It's okay. This one might be more helpful." Jackson scrolled to the image of Frost's tattoo, which had been documented at the same time as the mugshot.

Pham shook his head. "No. These are Chinese symbols. I would have remembered. This not the man."

Jackson loaded Buck Hinsic's mugshot, reminded of how much alike the two men looked. He could tell them apart but Pham might not. His own experience—backed up by academic studies—was that witnesses were better at identifying people of their own race.

Pham studied the image. "I think I saw him in restaurant once or twice."

"Eating a meal? Or in the parking lot?" The assailant could be a regular customer. Another bizarre irony.

"He eat." The old man shrugged. "If same guy."

Jackson showed him Hinsic's forearm swastika, and Pham's eyes sparked. "This could be tattoo. Dark and ugly. No art."

Now they just had to find Hinsic and bring him in. Maybe he and Frost had worked together on the recent hate crimes, and Frost had decided to save himself by blaming his partner.

That's helpful," Jackson said. "Thank you."

"I hope you find him."

"We will. But convicting him will be more difficult." On impulse, Jackson scrolled to the Jane Doe image in his own files and held it out. "Do you recognize this woman?"

Pham's eyes went wide, and he made a small noise of despair. "She's dead? Killed by same man?"

"Yes, she was murdered. And we're still investigating. Do you know her?"

The old man shook his head. "No. But she's like me. My heart hurts for her."

"Mine too." Jackson patted Pham's shoulder. "I'll be in touch."

After leaving the hospital, his first stop was a new two-story motel near Garfield. The nearly empty parking lot didn't mean much. In this area, the patrons were just as likely to arrive on foot, or bicycle, or by taxi. Sometimes drug dealers rented rooms just for a night or two, then their customers came to them in a central location where they could shoot up or snort their poison of choice and not have to risk carrying it anywhere.

Inside the narrow office, a young man sat behind the

counter, playing a game on his cell phone. He jumped to his feet. "Good morning, sir." His Indian accent was subtle and pleasant.

Jackson introduced himself, then pulled out his own cell. "I'm trying to identify this woman. She was assaulted and killed about a mile from here." He turned the image toward the clerk.

"She's dead?" The young man stepped back as if the photo were radioactive.

"Yes. And I need to know who she is. Do you recognize her?"

The clerk shook his head.

"Take a real look," Jackson snapped. He made a mental note to get more coffee.

The young man leaned in, shuddered, and shook his head. "I've never seen her. Why do you think she stayed here?"

"I'm just checking all the motels in the area."

"Good luck." The clerk glanced at his own phone again.

Jackson walked out feeling grumpy. This could turn out to be a waste of time.

He drove four blocks and parked at a rundown older motel with a neon sign missing the X in Texan. This time the clerk was an older woman with a short gray ponytail. Jackson was momentarily optimistic she would be more helpful. But as he said his name and rank, she looked him over and frowned. "We don't allow prostitutes or drug addicts here, so no, I can't help you."

Jackson showed her the victim's photo and forced himself to sound pleasant. "Have you seen this woman? She's been murdered, so it's important."

The clerk took his phone in her hands, startling him. Jackson wished he'd taken the time to get prints made at the department.

She stared at the image for a few seconds, then shook her head. "I don't know. She looks vaguely familiar."

"Will you check your records for the weekend? And see if she stayed here Saturday or Sunday night."

The woman gave him an odd look. "We don't take people's pictures when they check in."

He knew that! Jackson pulled in a quick breath. He had to get more caffeine ASAP. Four hours of sleep wasn't cutting it, and he was starting to think they'd given him decaf earlier. "Were you on duty Sunday night?"

"Yeah. Seven to seven on the noc shift. Ain't life grand?"

Jackson had a moment of compassion for her. A twelve-hour overnight shift in a sleazy motel had to be rough. It probably wasn't how this woman had visualized her retirement years. "That must be tiring. But what I meant was that I'd like you to check your guest list for Sunday night and see if any have a female Asian name." That was presumptuous. The victim could be named Kate Smith. But hell, he had to figure this out somehow.

The clerk looked at the noisy clock on the wall. "My shift is over in ten minutes."

"Then please get started."

She scowled, scrunching up her lined face. "I can't tell you a guest's name without some kind of warrant or something, can I?"

"She's dead. So in this case you can." Jackson glanced at the coffeepot on the end of the counter. Almost empty. *Damn.* He almost walked out. This was such a long shot. Even if the clerk came up with a female Asian name, it didn't mean she was the victim. But that would be easy enough to rule out.

"Are you gonna just stand here while I look? This could

take a while." The clerk was clearly irritated.

He remembered a coffee stand a few blocks away. "I'll be back in ten minutes." Jackson hurried out.

Walking would be quicker, he decided. And on foot, he could cut in front of customers who were lined up in their cars.

Still, the whole thing took longer than he'd anticipated. And on the return trip, a cyclist on the sidewalk nearly hit him. Jackson jumped out of the way and dropped his hot cup. The lid shot off and the coffee spilled all over the sidewalk. *Crap!*

Suddenly worried about the time, he jogged back to the motel, ignoring his incision pain. The night clerk was gone, and a younger woman stood behind the counter.

"Damn."

"I don't usually get that kind of response." The sort-of-pretty girl grinned.

Jackson forced himself to smile back. He hadn't meant to swear out loud. "What's the name of the clerk who just left?"

"Betty. Why? Is she in trouble?"

"She was helping me with something." Jackson started over, introducing himself, then showing the victim's photo. "Have you seen her before?"

The clerk grimaced. "No. Sorry. Most of our customers are short-term construction workers." She lowered her voice. "Or drug dealers. Plus a few prostitutes."

Like he thought. The desk phone rang, and the young clerk picked it up. When she got into a convoluted conversation about weekly rates versus daily rates, Jackson checked the time. He had to get going. He or another team member could follow up with the motels later—if they didn't get a response from the photo in the newspaper this morning.

Chapter 9

On the drive downtown, he stopped at Full City and bought coffee and pastries for the team, trying not to add up the money he'd spent on caffeine that morning. In his car, he tried to gulp some down but it was too hot.

At the department, he carefully carried his load upstairs and went directly to the conference room. He set everything down, opened his cup, and drank a third. He hoped to start feeling human in a few minutes.

Before that could happen, Sergeant Lammers strode in, grinned, and pointed at the carryout container. "Is one of those cups for me?"

Oh hell. He wasn't ready for this. "Uh, sure." He handed her Quince's half decaf with cream.

"You don't mind that I invited myself to your task force meeting?" Lammers let out what was supposed to be a laugh. "I won't stay long. I mostly wanted to let you know I set up a meeting with the local chapter of the Asian American Council."

Dread filled his stomach. "You mean with me?"

"Yep. They want some reassurance that our department can keep them safe. And since you have an unidentified victim, they might be able to help with the ID as well."

"I can accomplish both of those with a phone call."

"You're set to speak at their meeting this afternoon at four."

The only part of his job he hated.

Evans waltzed into the room. "Public speaking? Jackson's favorite." She laughed, winked at him, then reached for the cup with her initial on the lid. "Thanks."

"Last time I buy either of you coffee." Jackson walked to the end of the room with the whiteboard, pulled out his case notes, and started mapping out the crimes. He divided the board into three columns, then wrote *Vandalism, Pham*, and *Jane Doe* at the top. Under the first heading, he listed the three restaurants that had been targeted. For Pham, he added the names Ray Frost and Buck Hinsic, followed by the day and location of the attack. While he was adding to the murder-case column, he heard others come into the room. He turned to see Schak and Quince at the end of the table.

Their mismatched looks made his smile. Next to Schak's squat body and square head, Quince looked like a tall, handsome actor or model. As Schak took a seat, Evans passed him the last cup of coffee and shrugged at Quince. When the men had settled in, Jackson glanced at the clock on the wall. He was still waiting for a property-crimes detective.

Clare Upton rolled in a moment later, scooting her wheelchair up to the table. Middle-aged and lean, she hadn't let her new disability soften her. Jackson introduced the detective even though he suspected his team had all met her at least once.

"I'm glad to participate," she said. "But I don't have much time. Can we deal with the property issues first?"

"Of course. You have the floor."

Oops. Wrong cliché. Jackson smiled, hoping she hadn't noticed or cared.

"I've printed out our findings, but I'll summarize the gist of our investigation." She handed Quince a stack of papers to pass around. "The two restaurants previously targeted are the Angkor Cafe on Chambers and Eighteenth, and Lok Yaun on West Eleventh. The Angkor was tagged with graffiti on June twenty-first, and Lok Yaun was hit on June twenty-third with both graffiti and a broken window. None of the words or designs matched the signature of any known gang taggers." She paused and looked around the table.

"What was the window broken with?" Jackson asked, thinking about the club-like weapon used on the victims.

"A large rock was thrown through it. The act had to take considerable force, so the perp was either quite strong or high on meth or PCP." She glanced at her notes. "We questioned two members of the Southside Kings but made little progress. Now I'm hearing that a new white nationalist group might be responsible."

They had heard that from his and Evans' reports. So no help from her investigation.

"What about the Asian woman who was harassed?" Evans asked.

"We talked with two of her employees, and they think it was personal," Upton said. "A guy she had kicked out of her store earlier in the week. So we don't think it's a related incident."

But the two acts of vandalism probably were. "Did you collect any physical evidence at either scene?"

"Nothing that panned out."

"Did the perp paint any swastikas on the buildings?"

"No, but the number fourteen was featured several times." Upton frowned, seeming uncertain.

Jackson thought the symbol could be important. "What does that mean?"

Evans cut in to answer. "It stands for fourteen words. Do you want to hear them?"

Jackson nodded, knowing he actually didn't.

"We must secure the existence of our people and a future for white children."

"Nice." Schak shook his head in disgust.

Jackson concurred. But it was time to get back to the human beings who'd been assaulted—by the assholes who felt that way. "Anything else?"

"Not from me." The property-crimes detective met his eyes. "Can I go?"

"Yes. Thanks for your time."

When she'd left, he started with an update for those who had missed last night's arrest. "Buck Hinsic and Ray Frost are members of the Homelanders, a Portland-based white nationalist group with a chapter in Eugene. Evans located Frost at the Brewster, and we brought him in for questioning. He made a verbal slip that indicated he might be guilty of attacking Pham, but then he backtracked and eventually gave us Hinsic's name. Which is both strange and surprising." Jackson turned back to the board and underlined the man's name. "Frost says he's witnessed Hinsic assaulting both Muslims and Asians. I put out an ATL on him last night."

Schak scowled. "Is he a likely suspect or is Frost just shifting blame?"

Jackson was still asking himself that question. "Hinsic has a rap sheet, including assault, so yes, he's a good possibility. And maybe Frost, although a white nationalist, doesn't really condone the violence."

"So I can quit looking at mugshots?" Schak sounded hopeful.

"For now." Jackson decided to share his efforts that morning even though they hadn't paid off. He didn't want Evans wasting her time either. "I checked the two nearest motels this morning. A clerk at the Texan says the victim looked sort of familiar, but she couldn't remember a name. Then the clerk's shift ended and she disappeared. I'll follow up with her again this evening." Jackson glanced around the room. "Anybody have anything to add?"

Lammers spoke up. "Five people have already called the department this morning about the photo in the paper." She set down her coffee. "Two just wanted to complain that we ran an image of a dead person, but three said they might know her. Who wants the names for follow-up?"

Jackson nodded at Evans, and Lammers slid a piece of paper across the table.

"I also showed both suspects' mugshots to Pham in the hospital," Jackson added. "He thought he recognized the swastika tattoo on Hinsic's forearm."

"Did he sound definitive?" Evans looked hopeful.

"No."

"What have you got for me?" Schak asked.

"Check the security camera footage at the Golden Dragon restaurant. The owners tried to help us with that last night, but they've never done it before and were clueless."

Quince cut in. "What's my assignment?"

"Take the victim's photo to every Asian restaurant in west Eugene. That includes Thai food, that little Cambodian place, and Jung's Mongolian Grill."

Quince gave a soft laugh. "That will take a few days."

"Split the list with Schak if you need to. We have to ID this woman."

"What's left?" Evans asked.

"You can attend her autopsy this afternoon." Jackson grinned. "While I meet with the public." That would teach her not to be so amused by his PR assignments.

Evans groaned. "I'll trade you."

Lammers looked over at Evans and laughed. "No. I want Jackson to do the outreach. I told the group I'd send our lead investigator as well as a crime-prevention specialist." A phone rang in the sergeant's pocket. Lammers slipped it out and took the call, standing to walk out of the room as she did.

Jackson glanced around at his team. "Any other leads? Ideas?"

The silence unnerved him. Mostly because he felt stumped too. Lammers' voice in the hall caught their attention, and they all strained to hear.

Abruptly she hurried back in. "We have another death. A woman found in her own bed with no obvious cause." Lammers pointed at Evans. "Skip the Jane Doe autopsy and take the lead on this one. It could simply be an overdose."

Evans glanced at Jackson.

He was already there. "Does the case have to go to someone on my team? We have our hands full with these hate crimes."

"I don't make these decisions without good reason." Lammers was still standing. "The other task force is in court this week, hopefully securing a conviction in that triple murder." She gave Jackson a look that dared him to argue.

He didn't. But he wondered if, on some subconscious level, Lammers was dismissing his unidentified Asian-victim case as unsolvable. Maybe even unimportant. The thought pissed him off. He started to speak.

But Lammers cut him off and looked at Evans. "I'll text you the dead woman's name and address."

Digging in deeper, Jackson said, "Hey, if it's a real case, Evans shouldn't have to process the scene by herself. She might as well take Schak too." As soon as the words were out, he mentally kicked himself. Now he would be the one staring at surveillance footage.

"Great." Lammers glanced his way. "I guess that means you'll be doing both the autopsy and the PR outreach. Let me know how it all goes."

Not likely. Jackson took another big gulp of coffee. "Let's get to work. Then meet back here at five-thirty."

He gathered up his case notes, feeling overwhelmed and headed for failure. But at least the new death wasn't likely related to the hate crimes. He couldn't take any more of that.

Chapter 10

Evans turned down Schak's offer to ride out together. Regardless of what kind of case this new death turned out to be, they would likely need to split up to investigate. Besides, she'd done an intense workout that morning and was starving. She intended to grab a cheeseburger on the way out. And Schak wasn't supposed to eat fast food anymore. Poor guy.

The location Lammers had sent was in south Eugene in a neighborhood called College Hill, which wasn't really near the university. As she drove through the downtown area, her phone rang. *Todd.* Evans answered the call in her earpiece. "Good to hear from you."

"Hey, Lara. Someone has to keep our relationship going. You tend to disappear."

"I know. Sorry. We've had two new deaths in the last twenty-four hours, and we haven't even identified the first victim."

"Who's the second one?"

"A woman named Jola Shaffer, and Lammers assigned me the case."

"Any chance you have time to meet for lunch?"

"No. I'm headed to her death scene now. It's probably not a murder, but still, the sooner I get there, the better."

"What's the scenario? Can you tell me?"

"Not yet." She turned on Willamette and headed south.

"Let's try to meet for dinner. McMenamins at six-thirty?"

"Unless you only have a few hours. In which case I'll cook for you." He lowered his voice to a sexy whisper. "Then we'll have time for something else too."

"I'd like that. But I'll have to keep you posted."

"Just keep thinking about me. Naked. And ready."

Evans laughed and hung up. Todd was fun and the sex was good, but she couldn't get serious about him. They just didn't have enough in common. Todd was a county deputy who worked at the jail, so at least they had a shared law enforcement background. She'd accepted that she was only attracted to men in uniform, but they tended to be too socially conservative for her. Jackson, and maybe the fireman she'd dated recently, were the only exceptions . . .so far.

The home, located on a steep street, was smaller than the others in the neighborhood but had a wall of windows in front. Evans parked and stared up at the angular home, somewhat jealous. Her little duplex in the Bethel area lacked natural daylight. Maybe it was time to upgrade. She was making better money now and didn't intend to leave Eugene. She'd ended up here because the public safety department had offered her a job as an EMT. But after growing up in rural Alaska with alcoholic redneck parents, Eugene was like paradise.

She walked up the stone path and greeted the patrol cop standing on the front deck. The woman, about her age, nodded. "Officer Stubbs. First on the scene."

"Detective Evans. What have we got?"

"Jola Shaffer, age thirty-two. A friend found her dead this morning when she stopped by to pick Shaffer up for work."

"Where's the friend?"

"Sitting in her vehicle." The officer pointed at a compact car in the driveway. "I asked the woman to stay until a detective arrived, but she refused to wait in the house."

"I'll chat with her before I go in." Evans heard an engine and turned to see Schak park behind her car. "That's Detective Schakowski. Update him while I get the witness statement." Schak would head straight into the home to see the body.

As Evans approached the car, the grieving woman rolled down her window. Mascara had run down her face, and her nose was red. Still, she was young, attractive, and well-dressed.

"What's your name?"

"Amy Sarkota."

Evans asked her to spell it, then keyed the name into a note file on her phone. She preferred to use her tablet, but it was too cumbersome at times and the files synched up automatically anyway. "Can we go inside and talk?"

The woman shook her head. "Jola's body is in there, and I can't deal with that."

Evans decided not to force the issue. She'd questioned witnesses in stranger places. At least it was sunny and warm. "What is your relationship to Ms. Shaffer?"

"We're co-workers. And friends." Sarkota hiccupped as she struggled to control her emotions. "We carpool to work most mornings, and Jola is usually ready and waiting for me."

"What happened today?"

"She didn't come out of the house or respond to my texts, so I went up to the door. She didn't respond to my knocks either, so I went around back to see if she had slept in. Or something." The woman quietly burst into tears, then took a moment before speaking again. "The patio door off her bedroom was unlocked, so I stepped inside. Jola was in bed, but I could tell that something was really wrong."

Evans made a note of the door being unlocked. "Did you touch her?"

"No. I called her name, but she was so still I knew she was dead." Another sob. "I went straight back outside and called 911. I couldn't stay in the house."

Evans wished she'd taken a quick look at the body first. But Lammers had indicated the death might be an overdose. "Was Jola depressed?"

"Sometimes. She was going through a divorce."

A red flag. "Did she initiate the split?"

"Yeah. She'd been having emotional issues, and Jeff wasn't very supportive.

"That's her husband? What's his last name?"

"I'm not sure. No, wait. I think it's Griffen." The woman reached for a water bottle and took a long drink. "Can I go? I called my boss, but I still need to check in at work."

"Just a few more questions." Evans patted the witness' shoulder through the window. "Where are you both employed?"

"New Leaf. Jola is a massage therapist, and I administer hyperbaric oxygen treatments."

Evans started to ask what that meant, then changed her mind. She could imagine. Another new-age rip-off of people desperate to feel better. She moved to a more important issue. "Are you the one who reported that Jola's death might be an overdose?"

Another hiccup and a nod. "There was an empty bottle of vodka on her nightstand. And Jola takes Ambien to sleep sometimes too."

"Did she ever talk about suicide?"

The co-worker shook her head. "Jola wanted to be happy. She was getting counseling and meditating. And doing everything she was supposed to."

"Okay. You can go. But I need your phone number. I may have more questions."

Evans doubted she would need to talk to the witness again. The death sounded like an accidental overdose—which happened all the time. People overmedicated themselves in their effort to numb emotional pain. It was hard to use good judgment after a bottle of wine and/or a couple of tranquilizers.

As Evans walked away, the woman called out, "Oh, by the way. Her little dog is gone." The co-worker started to roll her car back toward the street.

Evans held up a hand to stop her and hurried back over. "What exactly does that mean? Did the dog run away when you opened the door?"

"No, it was already gone."

Huh. "Did you pick up Jola for work yesterday?"

"I did. And the dog was here. He's a terrier and his name is Scooter." The witness pressed her lips closed, then made a face.

She was holding something back. "What are you not saying? It could be important."

"Jola and her ex were fighting about the dog. Like a custody-issue thing."

Oh hell. Maybe this wasn't an overdose. "What do you know about Jeff Griffen?"

"Not much, except that he works at Hutch's."

"The bike shop?" Evans had seen the sign downtown near the election office.

"Yeah. I think he's a mechanic."

Evans was torn. She wanted more information about the husband, who was now a suspect, but she also had to get inside and look at the scene. "Thanks. I'll call you later with more questions."

The woman gave a sad wave and backed out.

Evans hurried toward the front door, then changed her mind. The co-worker said she'd gone around back, and Evans wanted to check out her version of events. And Schak was already inside taking note of everything. Thank goodness Jackson had sent him along. She knew he'd done it partly out of frustration, but also good leadership. When women died in their homes, it was almost always a man's fault. A troubled son. An angry ex-boyfriend. An obsessed stalker.

From the driveway, Evans headed down a flagstone path that cut between the garage and the tall hedge that served as a fence. At the back of the house, a short gate crossed the path. Evans easily opened it and walked into the backyard. *What was the point of the barrier?* Oh yeah, it would contain a small dog.

Reminding herself that this could be a crime scene, Evans stopped, pulled on latex gloves from her shoulder bag, then scanned the matching flagstone patio that ran the length of the back of the house. One set of barely-visible wet footprints faded after the first few steps. The shoe size looked small and narrow, like the prints belonged to a woman. Probably the co-worker who'd found the victim. Evans stepped carefully over to the first sliding door and discovered it was locked. A heavy curtain blocked the glass, but she guessed it led to a dining area or family room.

She backtracked to the outside edge of the patio and walked toward the second sliding door. After a careful scan of the patio area between her and the house, she pulled on booties and tiptoed across. With gloved hands, she reached for the sliding door—then stopped. A strand of hair dangled from the handle. Evans dug in her satchel for an evidence bag, then plucked and deposited the strand. She held the bag close to her face and examined the hair through the plastic. Medium brown, five inches long, slight curl. The co-worker, Sarkota, had short dark hair, so she hadn't left it. She suppressed a surge of excitement. The forensic evidence could be key to their investigation—or simply belong to the victim. Evans tucked the little bag away and pulled open the door.

Inside, Schak jumped and let out a startled noise. "Jesus, Evans."

"Sorry." She stepped into the room. "I was retracing the path of the co-worker who found her."

"And?"

"I found a strand of hair on the door handle." Evans glanced over at the woman on the bed. She was blonde. "And it didn't come from the witness or victim."

Schak made a grunting sound. "That could complicate things. On the surface, this looks like an accidental death."

"What have you got so far?"

"She's cold and stiff, so time of death is likely late last night. She has no visible signs of trauma or bruising. And the way she's positioned looks like she just fell asleep."

Evans stepped toward the bed and processed the details. A lean thirty-something woman, wearing a white T-shirt, with the lower half of her body still covered by a thin blanket. She had a pillow under her head and another lay next to her. At first glance, she seemed to be sleeping peacefully. But Evans had seen enough dead people to recognize the rigid lips and the odd paleness with a shadow undertone. She stepped back, pulled her phone, and took a few images for her own use. The medical examiner would take the official death-scene photos.

She turned to the nightstand, which held nothing but a digital clock. "Where's the empty vodka bottle?"

"I bagged it," Schak said. "Along with her phone and the empty bottle of Ambien that was just inside the drawer."

For a long moment, they were quiet. Evans ached for the loss of life. A woman who should have had another forty or so years left. How much emotional pain had she been in?

Near the front of the house, a door opened and soft footsteps sounded. *Probably the crime-scene techs*, Evans thought.

"What did the co-worker tell you?" Schak finally broke the silence.

"Shaffer and her husband were getting divorced, and they were fighting about who got to keep the dog."

"What dog?"

"The one that was here yesterday but gone this morning when she showed up."

"Uh oh. I guess we need to find the husband."

"Yep. And I know where."

Chapter 11

To keep busy until the autopsy, Jackson re-read the file on Buck Hinsic, the local leader of the Homelanders. A DUI, two meth-possession charges, and two assault convictions. Plus numerous parole violations. A career criminal—with a giant swastika on his forearm. At least Jackson knew who he was dealing with. And he couldn't stand the thought of the asshole, and likely killer, being out there somewhere, free to spread his special kind of negativity. Jackson had hoped a patrol officer would have arrested Hinsic already, but no one had. Impulsively he jumped up from his desk, deciding to make an attempt on his own.

The thug's last known address listed a house in the Bethel-Trainsong area. Jackson jogged down the outer stairs, visualizing the area and the home—probably the size of a two-car garage, built in the forties, with a buckled roof and peeling paint. Maybe with an old vehicle parked in the side yard, with weeds growing up around it.

As it turned out, he was mostly right. But the house was currently being renovated, and a team of roofers tossed faded tiles onto the ground below. Jackson walked up to the man standing in the driveway, talking on his phone. The guy, in his thirties and dressed too nicely for construction work, gave him a dirty look and turned his back. A moment later, the foreman had second thoughts, ended his call, and turned toward Jackson. "Uh, sorry. How can I help you?"

"Detective Jackson. I'm looking for Buck Hinsic. He used to live here."

"No clue. But I can give you the owner's name. He evicted the last tenants, then hired us to get the place into shape. It's a pigsty in there."

Jackson had no desire to go in and find out. He took the information, went back to his car, and made the call. The landlord picked up, sounding irritated. "What?"

"Eugene Police. I'm looking for Buck Hinsic. In connection with a homicide."

"I hope you find the son-of-a-bitch. He trashed one of my rentals and owes me a fortune."

"Any idea where he is?"

"No."

"Will you give me the name of his reference?" Guys like Hinsic often listed their own mothers because no one else would vouch for them.

"Thelma Hinsic, his sister. But I haven't been able to reach her."

"If you hear anything about him, please call the department. We need to find Hinsic."

"Good luck." The homeowner hung up.

Jackson got into his car and drove toward the old hospital downtown, where they performed autopsies. On the way, his phone rang, and he checked the ID: department dispatch. He pressed his earpiece and took the call.

"Officer Nolan just located and detained Buck Hinsic," the female supervisor said. "Do you want him brought to the department or booked into the county jail?"

Yes! About time. Jackson realized he might have to skip the autopsy. "Where are they now?"

"Third and Monroe. In the Whiteaker area."

That was close by. "Tell Nolan to stay put. I'm on my way there."

Jackson turned left and backtracked. Seven blocks later, he spotted two patrol SUVs parked in front of a decrepit two-story home. The officers were on the sidewalk, but their detainee was out of sight. Likely in the back of a unit.

Jackson parked and strode toward the patrol cops. He glanced in the back of the dark-blue SUV. A big guy with close-cropped dirty-blond hair was leaning forward, head down. Hinsic. Jackson continued up the sidewalk.

The younger officer stepped toward him. "Detective Jackson."

"Officer Nolan." The man had just completed Jackson's class on crime-scene procedure. "I want a few minutes with Hinsic now," Jackson said, "then you can take him to an interrogation room at the department."

"He's not feeling well." The older officer rocked on his feet.

What did that mean? "Is Hinsic in withdrawal?"

"Maybe."

Suddenly worried, Jackson spun back to the SUV and pulled open the door. The detainee moaned in pain.

"Hey. What's wrong?"

Hinsic turned his head without sitting up. Blood oozed from his nose and his eye was starting to swell. Jackson tensed, reminding himself not to draw any conclusions. "Are you okay?"

"Fuck no! Those assholes jumped me for no reason." The suspect spat blood.

"If you tried to run, they had a reason."

Hinsic finally sat up. "I never run."

Jackson decided to ask a few basic questions. "Where were you Sunday night? Between nine and midnight?"

"Why?"

"A security camera caught you near a homicide scene. What were you doing?"

"Fuck off!" The suspect's face contorted with rage, and his eyes blazed with a drug-induced intensity.

High on meth. No wonder they had to beat him to get him into the unit. Jackson pressed forward. "If one of your Homeland brothers participated in the assault, give me his name, and we'll go easy on you. The first one to talk gets the deal."

"I said fuck off!" With his hands cuffed behind his back, Hinsic lunged.

Jackson slammed the door closed. The officers stood behind him on the sidewalk, tense and ready.

"He's a piece of work," Nolan said.

Jackson nodded. "I changed my mind. Book him into jail so he can detox for awhile." Jackson gestured at the vehicle. "Then collect his blood from the backseat and send it to the crime lab for a DNA analysis."

"Yes, sir."

"Thanks."

On the way back to his car, Jackson glanced at his phone. He was definitely late now.

After wasting ten minutes finding a place to park, he took the elevator down to where they conducted autopsies in the basement. Surgery Ten. He opened the door, braced for backlash. As he pulled on a paper gown, the pathologist let out a harsh laugh. "What's the point, Jackson? I'm almost done here."

"Sorry. I had to speak with a murder suspect we just rounded up."

A moment of silence.

"For this homicide?" Rudolph Konrad's smooth skin made him look innocent, and his job had forced him to become detached—but a glimpse of grief played on the pathologist's face.

"Yes. We have a solid lead." Jackson stepped toward the table, blinking under the glare of the harsh overhead lighting. The stainless-steel cabinets and counters reflected streaks of light too, making the room feel surreal. And claustrophobic. It was bigger than an interrogation room but still windowless. And then there was the woman's dead body. Naked and splayed open down her chest. The smell of blood and bacteria was overwhelming. But something was off. The room was too quiet. Where was the medical examiner? After bringing in the bodies and prepping them for examination, he usually attended the post-mortem too. "Where's Gunderson?"

"Another death scene."

Oh right. The new case Lammers had assigned to Evans. For a moment, Jackson felt overwhelmed. The lull in his workload had lasted about five minutes. "Can you summarize your findings on this one for me?"

"Cause of death: brain bleed from three distinct subdural hematomas. Manner of death: homicide." Konrad glanced over. "Succinct enough for you?"

Jackson ignored the sarcasm. "Yes. Thanks. Anything of particular interest?"

"Yes and no. There's an interesting scar on her right hand that may have been caused by a curved knife. She had a combination of fish and rice in her stomach. And there were tiny lacerations under her fingernails."

Jackson's thoughts bounced around, but he focused on what seemed most important. "Any idea what caused the lacerations?"

"This is speculation, but it's possible the perp tried to scrape out his own skin tissue. If that's true, then she fought him at least briefly."

Were all criminals savvy about DNA now, thanks to CSI shows?

Konrad lifted an organ out of the woman's body cavity and set it on a scale.

Jackson tried not to wince. He usually arrived on time and left before this particular process started. "Any defensive wounds? Did she put up a fight?"

"Nothing visible. The blows were powerful. She may have seen the first one coming and grabbed his wrist. But after that, she had no chance."

"Any specs on the assailant?"

"A big guy. The blows came from almost directly above, so her attacker was at least eight inches taller than the victim, who is five-four." Konrad made a verbal note into his recorder, then turned back to Jackson. "And he's likely left-handed. Or at least he held the weapon with his left hand."

"What did he use?"

"I don't know. I found a few fragments in her hair, but I haven't analyzed them yet." Konrad removed another organ, put it on the scale, then motioned for Jackson to come closer. "See this abrasion? It might be post mortem."

"Her body was dumped?"

"I can't say for certain. But if so, it happened very soon after her death. Her livor mortis corresponds with the position of her body."

"Maybe she was killed inside a vehicle, then pushed out

onto the ground?" *Who would do that?* A boyfriend or a dealer.

"The first blow struck inside the car, then the next two while she was on the ground, just to make sure she was dead."

Konrad didn't usually speculate on that level of detail. "Will that hypothesis be established in your report?"

"In softer terms."

"Any help in identifying the victim? We still don't know who she is."

"Based on her stomach content and facial features, I'd guess that she's around thirty years old and mostly Southeast Asian. I say mostly because her hair color and texture indicate some European heritage."

Jackson hated that the distinctions mattered, but in the case of hate crimes, the person's physical characteristics were what triggered the fear and anger of the attacker. "By Southeast Asia you mean Cambodia, Laos, and Viet Nam?"

"Most likely." Konrad pushed his glasses back up. "But I'm not an expert in racial differences. And everything I read lately indicates that race is a cultural and political construct."

Jackson was starting to feel that way too. "I look forward to the day we all stop thinking and caring about it."

The pathologist cocked his head in skepticism. "Don't count on it. At least not until the entire older generation is gone."

Depressing thought. But the main question still remained. Why had the woman come here? Where was her family? "What about her uterus? Has she had any children?"

"No. But she does have a mild case of spina bifida. Another reason I think she might be from the peninsula."

Poor woman. A picture of her life was starting to form and it wasn't pretty. What was he forgetting to ask? "Uh, thanks. I'd better get back to work. Send me the full report as usual." Jackson stepped back and started to pull off his protective gear.

The pathologist shook his head. "Don't you want to know what else I found in her stomach?"

Chapter 12

Evans pulled into the parking lot behind the elections office. Hutch's, a bike shop, apparently didn't have any parking for cars. And the alley between the buildings served as a rest stop for homeless men. Schak had stayed to search the dead woman's home, but in her head she could hear him commenting about "the stink of piss in the morning." An older homeless guy whistled as Evans entered the bike shop. She strode up to the counter in the middle of the building, where a short middle-aged woman chatted with a customer. Feeling impatient, Evans moved toward the service area in the back. Three men, each at a mechanic station, focused on their repairs. "Jeff Griffen?" Evans called loudly.

The guy closest to her looked up. "How can I help you?" Tall, good-looking, and bone-thin, he could have passed for late twenties, but the gray at his temples suggested otherwise. The rest of his hair was light brown and hung around his neck in curls. A match for the strand she'd found on the sliding door.

"I'm Detective Evans. Can we talk somewhere private?"

"Uh, sure." Griffen wiped dark grease off his hands, then plodded over to the counter. "Deb, I'm going on break." Before his boss could respond, Griffen spun back to Evans. "We don't have a break room, so let's go outside."

As they walked out the side exit, Evans heard the other mechanics speculating in hushed voices. She turned to her suspect. "Let's get in my car. The alley smells bad."

Griffen turned back, stuck his head in the door, and yelled, "Piss cleanup in the alley. Q, it's your turn."

How often did they do that chore? Evans gestured at the suspect, wanting to get moving. "This way."

Inside her car, Evans locked the doors out of habit. Griffen tensed, then smiled, suddenly pouring on the charm. "Should I be worried?"

"Maybe." Evans turned to face him in the passenger seat. "Where were you last night? Anytime between seven and, say, three this morning?"

"Why? Do I need a lawyer?"

Cagey. "No, I'm just trying to establish your timeline. And your evasiveness doesn't look good."

"What's this about?"

"I'm asking the questions. We can do it here or in the interrogation room at the department. Where were you last night?"

He pulled in an extended breath as if to calm himself. "I was on a group ride until about seven. Then we had dinner at Tacovore. I got home around nine, watched TV for a while, then went to bed."

"Did you leave the house anytime after that?"

The man was silent for a full minute. Finally he blurted, "This is about the dog, isn't it? That bitch called the police, didn't she? Goddamnit!" Griffen slammed the dashboard.

Evans reassessed the situation, jumped out, and jogged around to the passenger side. She yanked open the door. "Get out and put your hands on the roof."

"What?" His mouth hung open, and he looked both irritated and worried. "I'm sorry. That won't happen again."

"Get out!"

He grudgingly complied.

"Turn around and put your hands on the roof."

"This isn't necessary," Griffen whined. "I can explain the whole thing calmly, I promise."

Evans searched him for weapons, then cuffed him.

"Am I under arrest?"

"Not yet. I'm just taking you in for questioning and keeping myself safe."

She opened the sedan's back door and gave Griffen a gentle push. He was too tall for her to guide him, and he whacked his head as he climbed in. "Ouch!"

"We'll talk at the department."

On the drive over, she called Schak to update him, and he agreed to meet her. At the department, Evans took the suspect into an interrogation room and told him to sit.

"I think I should call my lawyer."

She didn't want him to do that. Time for good-cop mode. "We should be able to clear this up quickly if you just answer a few questions. Can I get you some coffee?"

"No. But you can call my boss and tell her why my break is taking so long."

"I'll do that. Be right back." She closed the door behind her, and it locked automatically.

On the way upstairs, she called the bike shop and left a brief message. It wasn't her job, but whatever helped the suspect relax. In the break room, she ran into Schak. He was stuffing the last of bite of a sandwich into his mouth.

"So?" he said, chewing while talking. "It's past lunchtime."

"I didn't say anything."

"But I see the look in your eyes."

"You're hallucinating. And I had a cheeseburger earlier, so I make no judgments."

"Good. Cuz I'm putting sugar in my coffee too." He poured a cup and dumped in at least a tablespoon.

But at least he wasn't putting bourbon in his thermos anymore. Evans grinned. "I'm not your wife, so get over it." She filled a cup of water for herself and headed for the door.

"Slow down," Schak called, hurrying after her. "I have new information from a patrol officer."

Evans turned. "What?"

"A neighbor says she heard the couple fighting last night around nine-thirty."

That was solid. "She saw Griffen? Placing him at the scene?" Evans headed down the stairs.

"Yep. She says the argument was heated, but she doesn't really know what it was about."

"He already mentioned their dog, so I'll take the lead to start. This will be interesting." Evans activated the camera, then entered the interrogation room.

Griffen sat upright, a look of defiance on his face. "Did you call the shop?"

He sure was worried about his job. "Yeah, I called. Let's get started."

After the introductions, Evans got right to the heart of the issue. "Did you take the dog from your ex-wife's home last night?"

"She's still my wife. The divorce isn't final yet."

"Answer the question."

"Yes. It was supposed to be my week, but she had refused to let me have Scooter."

"Tell us what happened and be specific."

"After dinner with the bike club, I stopped by Jola's and tried to talk to her about being fair." Griffen seemed to shudder with frustration. "But she completely reneged on our agreement and said she was keeping Scooter."

"How did you react?" Evans hoped he would lie.

"I took the dog from her and left." His face and tone were deadpan.

That was one version of events. "Did she resist?"

"She yelled at me but I ignored her."

"Did you raise your voice?"

"Not really."

"So you just overpowered her with your strength?" Evans tried to keep her voice and expression neutral. The hardest part of the job for her.

Griffen scowled. "I don't like how you phrased that. I didn't overpower her because once I put my hands on Scooter, she gave up. Probably to protect the dog. He's tiny and gets pretty nervous."

Evans bit back several comments. This guy was a piece of work. And she strongly suspected he'd suffocated his wife. She let Schak take it from there. He had the eyewitness testimony.

"No harsh words, huh?" Her partner made a point to sound skeptical.

"Oh, we argued, but that was normal for us." Griffen shifted and groaned. "Can we take these cuffs off, please? I'm not a criminal, and I don't like being treated like one."

Arrogant too. Evans wanted to *tsk-tsk* him, but she didn't. "I'll move the cuffs to the front, but considering your earlier outburst, I'm not leaving your hands free." She got up and walked around behind their suspect.

Schak pressed his point. "Your neighbor heard loud shouting. She says you threatened Jola."

"Hey, I didn't mean any of it. I was just upset about losing my pet."

Evans re-cuffed Griffen in front while he shook his head. "Jola may have wanted the dog, but I took care of him. He's bonded to me."

Still standing, Evans locked on the suspect's eyes from two feet away. "What exactly did you threaten her with?"

Silence.

"Keep in mind that your neighbor already told me what she heard," Schak added.

Evans sat down, and they waited him out.

Finally Griffen said, "I know I was out of line. But this has been really hard for me. First Jola announced out of nowhere that she wanted to end our marriage. Then she asked me to move out—as soon as possible! Then wouldn't let me take the dog. Such bullshit!"

"I know divorce is rough." Schak's tone was surprisingly soft. "But this is important. What did you threaten?"

Another long silence. "I don't have to tell you anything. In fact, I want to call a lawyer."

Experience had taught them to wait, so they did.

Griffen glanced back and forth between the two. "I can't believe that bitch is making such a big deal of the dog. We can work it out."

For a moment, Evans thought he might not know his estranged wife was dead. But suspects lied and feigned ignorance all the time. And this guy was a manipulator. "You're saying Jola was fine when you left the house?" Evans asked.

"Yes, of course."

A lie for the camera. "What time was that?"

"Nine-thirty or so. Maybe a little later."

Schak cut in. "What kind of vehicle do you drive?"

"A Jeep Wrangler. I commute mostly by bike, but I do a

lot of camping and mountain biking too. Why do you want to know?"

"We're still expecting more witnesses to come forward," Schak said, his voice deadpan. "And we know you fought with the victim. Maybe you should tell us what really happened."

"Victim?" Griffen's eyes were frantic. "Is Jola saying I hit her? Because it wasn't like that. Well, not exactly. I mean, I grabbed her arm. And yes, maybe too tightly. But she bruises easily."

Given enough time, he would eventually tell them everything.

"What is Jola saying? Did she press charges? I have a right to know what I'm accused of."

He was quite the actor.

"Jola isn't the one pressing charges." Schak leaned forward. "And you know that. Because you killed her."

Griffen's mouth dropped open, and he made a strange moaning noise.

Evans jumped in, trying to soften the accusation and give him the out he needed. "We know you came back after the fight to confront her again. Maybe actually take the dog this time." Evans could finally see the whole scenario in her mind now. "You found Jola in bed, passed out from booze and pills. Maybe you thought she might already be dead. An act of suicide. So you helped her along, thinking it was what she wanted."

The suspect shook his head. "I'm not saying anything else without a lawyer."

Chapter 13

Back at his desk, Jackson pulled out the evidence bag and stared at the small silver key. The victim, still unidentified, had swallowed it as one of the final acts of her life. She clearly hadn't wanted someone to find it. But who? Her attacker? It seemed unlikely she would've had the time or focus to make the key disappear during an assault. The pathologist indicated that the perp was big and the attack had been violent and likely sudden. Jackson tried to visualize the scene in slow motion. If the key had been in the victim's hand or pocket when the stranger approached her, she might have had time between seeing the assailant coming at her and his first blow.

But what was so important to her?

The key looked too fragile for a safe deposit box. More likely, it fit a personal jewelry box or something similar. If that were the case, the victim had been protecting something personal. A thought hit him. What if the key accessed a money or drug stash? And she had known her attacker? Jackson remembered the pathologist's suggestion that the perp had killed the woman in his car, then dumped her. That didn't quite match the theory that she'd been targeted in a hate crime by a white nationalist. Or perhaps it did. Maybe the attacker had picked her up because she was Asian. Was their Jane Doe a prostitute? Another avenue to check out.

Jackson let out a sigh. Without knowing who the victim

was, narrowing down the motivation would be impossible. Unless she had been targeted just for her Asian appearance. Which had seemed more likely—before he knew about the key. Meanwhile, he had two skinheads in custody and no leverage with either. Unless they could get a DNA match between Hinsic and any trace evidence found on the victim's hands.

The analysis could take a week or more at the state lab unless he pressed for urgency, which he only did if he thought other victims were at stake. A stab of panic ran through his gut. More attacks could be coming. Jailing Frost and Hinsic might actually make things worse. The Homelanders had other members who might carry out attacks to avenge the arrests of their brothers. If the white nationalists were on a mission to intimidate people of color, they probably wouldn't stop with Asians. Other minorities could be next.

Frustrated, Jackson stood. Lammers had pulled half his team to investigate a non-related case. So Schak had turned over the surveillance footage from the restaurant to the crime lab to sift through. But the technicians might not prioritize it. They were working other cases too. And so far, the calls they'd received about the victim's photo were from the usual attention-seekers. Jackson glanced at the time. His meeting with the association was starting in twenty minutes. As much as he dreaded the encounter, he hoped the group might help him ID the victim. Or maybe the key.

As he left his cube, Evans called.

"Hey, what's up?" Jackson started down the outside stairs.

"My new case could be a homicide. The couple is in the middle of a divorce, and they're fighting over a dog."

"Sounds ugly. And time-consuming."

"It is. Sorry, but it means Schak and I have to stay on this one," Evans said.

"Okay. Thanks for the update.

"Are we still meeting at five-thirty?"

"Unless something breaks before then."

Jackson double-checked the address Lammers had given him. Shelton-McMurphey. Oh yeah, that new short street that connected Skinner Butte Park with the east end of the Whiteaker neighborhood. Other than the historic house on the hill, the area only had one other building.

A few minutes later, he pulled in and stared at a huge structure with intense red and gold paint. It looked more like a renovated warehouse than an office space. Did he have the location correct? Jackson went inside, realized he was in a health-food retail store, and turned around. He tried another entrance and ended up in a hallway with a lot of doors. Resisting the urge to simply leave, he headed toward the center of the building. A woman came out of a room and intercepted him. "Are you Detective Jackson?"

"I am." He held out his hand.

"Eva Chung." Thirty-something, petite, and quite pretty, she gestured for him to come inside.

Jackson followed her into a long, narrow conference space. He quickly scanned the table, counting ten people. A smaller group than he'd anticipated. Thank goodness.

"We rent this room to meet once a month," Chung said. "It's less hassle than leasing our own space." She turned to the members and introduced him. Jackson forced himself to smile. This would be over soon.

He gave a quick overview of the task force's progress on the hate crimes, then reported the arrest of the two

Homelanders. Several people sighed in relief, and others patted the shoulders of the people next to them.

"But we're far from a conviction," Jackson cautioned. "The suspects are being held in the county jail on minor offenses. So they'll likely be released." He hated saying that out loud and tried not to look at the disappointment on their faces. "I'll meet with the district attorney soon to see if he's willing to file charges, but we need more evidence."

"Like what?" Chung asked. "You have an eyewitness."

"Mr. Pham's assailant wore a bandana, so we actually don't." He needed to change the subject. "Most important, we haven't identified the murder victim yet. Did you see her image in the newspaper this morning?" He glanced around the room.

The man nearest him spoke up. "We did. And we discussed it already. None of us know her." His voice was surprisingly deep for his small frame.

Crap. Jackson suppressed his disappointment. "Have you reached out to the rest of your members?"

"Yes. And we still hope to hear something positive," Chung said. "We'll call you if we do."

What now? He really needed help. And his team knew so little about the victim.

"What was she wearing?" an older woman asked. "The photo doesn't show us."

He started to ask why it mattered, then stopped and visualized the scene. "A light-brown shirt with short sleeves. And black pants. Probably made of cotton." Jackson shook his head. "Actually, I don't know the fabric. I just know it didn't feel stretchy."

"Traditional Viet clothing." The older woman nodded solemnly.

Was that helpful? "Is that important? I need to know."

"It means she probably bought the clothes in Viet Nam. So she hasn't been in this country all that long. Or maybe she goes home to visit and shop."

Maybe the motel clerk had seen her. He would definitely check back.

Eva Chung spoke up again. "Was she wearing any jewelry?"

"No." Jackson remembered the key and dug it out of his satchel. "But this was in her stomach. Any idea why or what it unlocks?" He handed the evidence bag to the older woman who had asked about the clothes. As long as the key didn't leave his sight, he wasn't breaking the chain-of-evidence protocol.

She looked it over. "This probably belongs to a small box or file that holds personal items. Important papers, or maybe even the personal effects of someone who's now in the spirit world." She looked over at Jackson. "But I'm guessing."

Spirit world? Jackson didn't want to know. "Any idea why she might swallow it?"

"To safeguard the spirit, of course."

Chapter 14

Earlier that day

Sophie finished the first draft of her unidentified-murder-victim story and checked the word count. Too short. But she had so little information. She went back into the file and added a couple of lines about the earlier vandalism incidents at the Asian restaurants—without specifically connecting the crimes. But she knew it was lazy reporting. She called Jackson and left him a message: "Hey, would you call me please? I need to know if Jane Doe's murder was a hate crime. And if you know her name yet. And whether her death is linked to the vandalism incidents. I can help you with this one if you keep me in the loop."

She reached for her tea, realized she didn't have any, and went to the little kitchen area to make some. It wasn't technically a break room—they'd lost that little bonus when the publisher moved the shrinking newspaper staff upstairs—but they still had a small fridge and a microwave. She was grateful for that. And happy to still be employed. Many of her friends weren't. The sports-writing staff was still intact, but half of the copy for the rest of the paper was now written by unpaid interns.

Back at her cubicle, she opened the article she was writing about an environmental lawsuit filed by teenagers. Technically, it fit under the subject of courts, so she was keeping busy with it, hoping not to be assigned something dull and mandatory.

Her cube neighbor, who covered business news, stuck her head over the wall. "That tea smells good. Is it mint?"

"Always. I make it every day."

"I've never noticed before."

Abruptly, her boss walked up, his wild eyebrows twitching. Hoogstad was obviously worked up about something. "Grab your camera, Sophie, and get down to the county courthouse. Dennis McCarthy is giving a stump speech, and protestors showed up. I sent an intern down there to cover it, but this could get ugly."

"What kind of protestors?" She was already on her feet and lunging for her bag. McCarthy, the state's new governor, had recently announced he was running for the presidency, but he wasn't popular in Eugene.

"I don't know." Hoogstad gestured for her to hurry. "We need copy and images, especially if anyone gets arrested. Go!"

Sophie poured her tea into a thermos, grabbed her sweater, and jogged down the stairs. She hoped the excitement, whatever it was, didn't dissipate before she got downtown.

With little traffic on the expressway, the mid-morning drive went quickly. She parked in a loading-only zone and bolted across the street. The oncoming car honked, and Sophie waved. On the corner, a crowd of about two hundred people had gathered in the plaza in front of the courthouse/county admin building. She looked up to the top of the steps but didn't see a public speaker. In the crowd, small groups of onlookers shouted at each other. On the right and bunched up near the front, the attendees carried simple pro-McCarthy signs. The group on the other side and a few clusters in the back held up posters with bold political questions meant to challenge the candidate.

Where was McCarthy?

Sophie pushed through the crowd, shouting "Excuse me" over and over, until she reached the front. Three police officers stood at the bottom of the steps, occasionally shouting at attendees to stay back. Sophie took several photos of the crowd and the cops interacting. She stepped toward the uniformed woman in the middle. "Officer, what's happening? When is McCarthy coming out to speak?"

"Any moment."

Sophie thanked her and headed through the crowd. She wanted to talk to the people in the back with the banner that read: *How many people have you killed?*

The two guys and one young woman holding the sign looked college-aged. After snapping a couple of photos, she approached the taller of the young men. "Hi. I'm a news reporter. What does your sign mean? Why do you think McCarthy has killed people?" It had to be a metaphor or some indirect responsibility issue.

"He's a military man who's served in a lot of wars," the tall guy said. "We didn't vote for him as governor, and we definitely don't want a neocon to be President."

"You're afraid he'll start a war?" Sophie directed her question to the whole trio.

"My uncle knows him," the stocky guy said. "They fought in Nam together, and Uncle Rick says he's a coward."

Suddenly intrigued with the candidate, Sophie decided to write a political profile—if she could get an interview—and sell the freelance piece to the Portland paper. "Will you give me your uncle's name and number? I'd like to interview him."

The stocky kid laughed. "He'll be so conflicted. He hates reporters, but he hates McCarthy even more." The kid looked up the number in his phone and shared it with Sophie. She glanced at the two others who were holding the sign. "What else do you know about McCarthy and why are you opposed to him?" She would have to vet all their information, but at least she had a hook and a direction for the protestors-at-the-rally piece her boss wanted.

"Besides being a hawk, he's too socially conservative. He wants stricter drug laws and looser gun control." The tall kid gestured with a finger twirl. "Crazy!"

"Do you know anything about him personally?"

The stocky guy jumped in again. "My uncle's been following his political career over the years. I'm pretty sure he's married and has a son who's campaigning for him."

Sophie made a note of both. "Thanks." She started to walk away, then turned back. "What branch of the military was McCarthy in?"

"Army," the kid offered. "He retired as a colonel."

"I appreciate the information."

The candidate's voice suddenly boomed over the loudspeakers. "Thank you all for coming! Even those who don't support me."

Sophie headed back to the front, still hoping for something newsworthy.

"I'm Dennis McCarthy, and I want to be your next President!"

The crowd on the right roared, blasting her ears. Sophie dug in her bag for earplugs. They only softened the volume but it was worth it. The candidate launched into a list of what he thought was wrong with the country, but Sophie didn't take notes. She could check his website for policy information. She tuned out what he was saying and focused on the man. Casually dressed in dark pants and a white shirt with rolled-up sleeves and no tie. But at sixty-something, he was still buff and filled out every inch of the shoulders and sleeves. Close-cropped gray hair and a semi-attractive face, despite the pouch sags on both cheeks. He gestured with his arms occasionally but didn't point his finger. She liked that.

McCarthy transitioned to talking about the justice system, mass incarceration, and the push for reform. "I have two sons," he announced. "One is a law enforcement officer and one is a prisoner. They were raised in the same home so their life choices are theirs alone."

A criminal son? Sophie started taking notes again.

"So I know and understand both sides of this issue. And I'm here to tell you I will veto any legislation that softens our laws, including drug laws. Criminals have to be held accountable."

The supportive crowd cheered. Someone started to chant "Lock them up!" and others joined in. The candidate let a small smile creep onto his face for the first time. As he raised an arm to quiet the crowd, something flew through the air and splatted against his white shirt. The crowd gasped as the red stain of tomato juice dripped down his chest.

Another tomato flew and smashed into his belly.

The two male officers bolted into the group on the left, shouting, "Who threw that?"

Sophie rushed forward and snapped pictures of the startled and stained candidate. In that moment, his face held a controlled rage. But she was being paid to take pictures of protestors being arrested. So she whipped around and followed the officers into the crowd. Behind her, McCarthy ranted about the rule of law as his supporters chanted, "Lock them up!"

Sophie reached the back of the crowd. A scruffy young

man was on the ground, and a police officer had one knee on his back as he cuffed him. Sophie managed to snap a few pictures before the second officer yelled, "Get back! No photos!"

Sophie hurried into the crowd, not wanting to have her camera seized. But their effort to control the public narrative was laughable. Everyone in the crowd had a camera in their phone. The only difference was that she had direct access to a news publication.

Chapter 15

At his desk, Jackson ordered pizza for the team, spent a few minutes reading up on Viet culture, then called his daughter. Katie didn't answer so he texted her: *Dinner with task force then work for a few hours. Home at eight or so.*

He tried calling Kera too, with the same result. So he re-typed the same message and sent it to Kera. A flash of panic hit him as he visualized himself responding inappropriately later on to his daughter, thinking she was his girlfriend. That might not be the right term for his relationship with Kera since they weren't having sex, but they were raising kids together. Calling her his partner wasn't right either. That's how he referred to Schak.

Jackson refocused his thoughts, opened his case notes, and read through them. The task force meeting was starting in ten minutes, and he felt totally unprepared. Mostly because he'd made no real progress. He hoped Quince or a tech had found something useful on the video footage from the security cameras. Schak and Evans would probably be no help at all. But if they already had the victim's husband in custody, they might have some time for his case in the next few days.

Evans was already in the conference room when Jackson arrived. As he walked past, he impulsively touched her shoulder. A spark shot through him, rattling his nerves. *Damn. Never again.* He had to get beyond his physical attraction. He was a family man, and Evans had no interest in being a mother. Kera, on the other hand, was perfect for him and his family. And he loved her too.

"Hey, what's up?" Evans asked. "Are you okay?"

Jackson forced himself to focus. "Just frustrated by this case."

"Still no ID?"

"No, but I think a motel clerk remembers the victim and lied to me. I plan to see her again this evening."

"I'll be working late too." Evans reached for her water bottle. "Our suspect lawyered up, so we had to release him."

"The Leeds trial will be over soon, and we'll both get more help." Jackson glanced at the whiteboard and realized they needed a second one. "I'll be right back."

He hustled down to the supply room and grabbed the wheeled board they had used at the old building. When he pushed it into the conference room, Schak and Quince had arrived but were still standing.

"You ordered food, right?" Schak had a wild look in his eye. "Because I missed lunch and I'm not staying if you're not gonna feed us."

Jackson smiled at the empty threat. "Pizza is coming."

"Yes!" Schak sat down. "Terry made a gluten-free, low-fat version the other day, and I swear, not even the dog would eat it."

Evans rolled her eyes. "You don't have a dog." She got up, grabbed the small whiteboard from Jackson, and rolled it to the front. "Should I start filling this in?"

"Let's update the Jane Doe homicide first." Jackson glanced at Quince. "That might only take about three minutes."

Quince shook his head. "I got nothin'. The attack was out

of the security camera's line of sight, and not a single Asian restaurant recognized her as an employee." He drummed his fingers. "But I only talked with eight businesses within a two-mile radius of the scene. I can expand the search tomorrow."

"I hope you won't have to." Jackson moved toward the main board. "I think a motel clerk has information, and I intend to get it." He wrote *Texan Motel* low on the board under the Jane Doe column. At the top, he wrote *Key*, then turned to the group.

"What key?" Evans asked.

Jackson pulled the evidence bag from his satchel and passed it to Evans. "The pathologist found this in the victim's stomach."

"That's weird." Quince made a face.

"She had something to hide," Evans commented. "Something she wanted to keep safe."

"That suggests she knew her attacker." Schak was suddenly paying more attention. "So maybe it's not a hate crime."

"I'm not assuming that," Jackson countered. "Because no one else seems to know this victim, including the Asian council group." He remembered what they'd said about a spirit. Jackson hesitated to bring it up, but it likely contradicted Schak's theory. "Someone at the Asian council suggested that the key was to a box that the victim believed held a spirit."

"Even weirder," Quince said.

"Or something that belonged to a loved one," Jackson added. His brief research earlier on Viet culture had helped him understand. "Viet people believe that ancestors take a spirit form after death, and they try to keep those loved ones close to them."

"So she swallowed the key to keep the spirit close?" Schak scratched his head. "Because she knew she was going to die?"

"Something like that." Jackson didn't fully understand either. He barely knew what he believed.

Evans scoffed. "Maybe she was just protecting her valuables." She paused for a moment, then laid out a scenario. "What about this? She probably didn't know the perp, but she saw him coming at her. And obviously she had the key with her. She maybe even had her ID and her phone. Which meant he would have access to everything if she died. So she swallowed the key to keep the thug from ransacking her place and taking what was in the box."

They were all quiet for a moment.

"Interesting possibility," Jackson finally said.

"Hey, just brainstorming." Evans sounded a little defensive.

"The pathologist suggested that our Jane Doe might have been attacked in the perp's vehicle, then dumped out moments later." He'd given the scenario some thought. "That would suggest at least a transactional acquaintance between the two."

Jackson's phone rang in his jacket pocket. He slipped it out and checked the ID. Someone at the crime lab. He took the call and put it on speaker. "Jackson here. At a task force meeting."

"It's Jasmine Parker."

Jackson recalled the brief image he'd seen on Sophie's phone the night he'd been called to the scene. Even if it had been Parker, the relationship didn't matter. As long as she didn't leak any critical information to her reporter girlfriend. A dark thought flashed. What if that was how Sophie seemed to always have inside information?

Jasmine started talking and he tuned her in, eager to hear details.

"We finished searching the trash bags we collected at the crime scene. And didn't find anything useful."

"No ID? No weapon?" He had to ask.

"No, but after coming up empty, I went back to the area today to do a daylight search. And I found a room-key card for the Texan Motel."

Yes!

"The card's black and it was under the dumpster, so I'm not surprised we missed it that night."

He'd known the clerk was lying. Or at least trying not to get involved. "Great news. Thanks for going the extra mile." He decided his earlier speculation was irrelevant. Parker was the best tech they had.

"Sorry that's all we came up with."

"Thanks for the update."

The crime-scene tech ended the call.

Jackson glanced at Quince. "I'll check back at the Texan tonight. Hopefully, we won't need a subpoena."

Evans cut in. "If she was staying at a motel, and no one local recognizes her, do we assume that our victim is new to the area?"

Jackson nodded. He'd been toying with that idea from the beginning. "And she might have just arrived from Viet Nam. Apparently her clothes are traditional in the Viet culture and were likely purchased there."

"And our country welcomes her with a hate-crime murder." Evans shook her head. "I think I prefer the angry boyfriend/husband scenarios. At least I understand those emotions."

Another silence in the room.

Before Jackson could suggest moving on to the new case, someone knocked on the door. A moment later, the front-desk officer walked in with a large pizza box. She looked at Jackson. "You owe the slush fund twenty-six dollars."

He had the cash on him so he handed it over as his teammates dug into their dinner. He helped himself to a slice, and the room was quiet except for the sound of Schak moaning in pleasure.

Evans finally looked over at Jackson. "Our turn?"

"Yes. Let's keep moving."

She wiped her hands, picked up a marker, and walked to the small whiteboard. Across the top she wrote *Jola Shaffer, 32*, then created three columns below. In the first section, she wrote *No visible trauma.* In the middle column, Evans noted *Getting divorced, fought over dog.* At the top of the third area, Evans penned *Suspects*, then listed *Jeff Griffen, husband, mechanic at Hutch's.*

"A dog?" Quince's mouth hung open. "She was killed over a pet?"

Jackson shared the sentiment. He had a scar above his eyebrow from a dog bite and had encountered more than his share of unpleasant canines on the job, including some that had killed a young woman.

"People take their pets very seriously." Evans raised her eyebrows in mock surprise. "Our suspect admits that he showed up at his wife's house around nine p.m. and aggressively took the dog from her arms. But he claims he left immediately after, and that she was fine."

"A neighbor confirms the confrontation," Schak added. "But she didn't see the husband leave."

"With no obvious trauma, what's your theory about how

he killed her?" Jackson asked. He hadn't seen the crime-scene photos and probably wouldn't.

"Suffocation." Schak and Evans said it at the same time.

Evans took it from there. "We suspect Griffen left, then came back and found his wife sleeping heavily. She'd been drinking vodka and possibly took Ambien too. He could have simply put a pillow over her face long enough to kill her."

Jackson didn't see the motivation. "But he already had the dog. Maybe she just got depressed and simply overmedicated."

"Possibly." Evans nodded. "But Griffen still faced both a divorce and a custody fight in court. And maybe he stood to lose financially too. He wouldn't be the first man to kill his wife rather than go through a divorce."

Schak muttered something under his breath. When Jackson looked at him for clarification, his partner smiled sheepishly. "Most important, the husband called a lawyer and pleaded the Fifth, which is never a sign of innocence."

Jackson held back a sigh. The husband/boyfriend, or *intimate partner* as sociologists labeled them, was almost always guilty. "We need to canvass the neighborhood for witnesses and hopefully establish exactly when Griffen left." Jackson couldn't help but make suggestions. He was used to running homicides.

"We will." Schak rubbed his hands over the stubble on his head. "But I'm still looking at her phone calls and social media posts."

"I'll go door-to-door after this meeting," Evans added. "But what Schak is trying to say is that we need more people."

"I'll talk to Lammers." Jackson didn't know what good it would do, but sometimes the boss helped out when they were shorthanded. "She won't likely go out and question witnesses, but she might write up subpoenas or check financial docs."

Evans looked relieved. "Good. We need paper to get Griffen's phone records. That might be the only way to pin down his location at the time of death."

"Did Gunderson give you a rough estimate for TOD?" Jackson asked.

"Between ten and midnight, but the autopsy is tomorrow morning."

"Let's stay open-minded," Jackson said. "We may learn that her death was self-induced. After her ex took the dog, she may have gotten depressed and overmedicated."

Schak nodded. "There was an empty bottle of vodka *on* her nightstand and a prescription for Ambien *inside* her nightstand." He grimaced. "Too bad we won't have bloodwork results for several days."

Jackson remembered Evans had already released Griffen. "Can we pick up the husband on some other charge? I'd feel better if he was in custody."

Evans shrugged. "He has a clean record."

"Nobody's perfect. Let's talk to the victim's friends and family and see what they have to say about Griffen."

"Oh shit." Evans looked mortified. "I haven't even notified the next-of-kin yet."

"Then let's get going," Jackson said. "This will be another long night."

Chapter 16

Sophie ate an apple at her desk while she checked out Dennis McCarthy's website, then called the contact number listed. "Hey, this is Sophie Speranza with the *Willamette News*. I was at Mr. McCarthy's speech this morning, and I'd love to give him some better coverage. Can we set up an interview? Let me know." She recited her phone number and ended the call. She didn't expect him or his staff to respond. But she always asked for what she wanted. It was the only way to succeed.

She opened a new file and wrote the lead sentence for her report about the political rally: *As a throng of supporters chanted "Lock them up," in response to candidate McCarthy's position on crime, two men in the crowd threw tomatoes.*

An editor might recast it, but maybe not. But she couldn't make herself lead with the tomatoes. Most people would only see images from the rally on the nightly news or on Facebook. As a print journalist, she had to give readers more context.

"Tell me you got pics of McCarthy today!" Her boss was suddenly in her cube and quite excited.

"Of course." She just hadn't processed them yet. "I'll upload them now. I had an idea for a lead on this story, and I wanted to get it into a file before I lost track of it."

"Show me." Hoogstad stepped behind her and leaned over her shoulder.

Sophie enlarged the text, hoping he would give her some space. She could smell pastrami and mustard on his breath.

"Excellent." He patted her shoulder, and she tried not to recoil from the touch. He meant well.

"Thanks." Sophie rolled her chair sideways to look at him. "If I write an in-depth profile on McCarthy, will the paper run it?"

"Only if you make him look good. We're under new ownership, and you know they have a bias."

"That's what I thought." She would sell the piece to the Portland paper. "Let me get on these photos. You're gonna like them. I caught his red-stained white shirt before he bolted."

"If they ever lay you off, Sophie, I'm quitting in protest." Hoogstad laughed. "Kidding. But I do love your work."

His praise stunned her. A surge of pride followed.

After he walked away, her cube neighbor popped up, eyes wide in mock surprise. "I'm your witness. I heard him say it."

"Thanks." Sophie grinned. "For a moment, I thought I was hallucinating."

She rolled back in front of her computer, plugged in her camera, and started the upload. When it completed, she opened a browser and googled the phrase *Dennis McCarthy sons*. Only a few relevant links showed near the top of the results. She opened the second one, published by her own newspaper a few years before her time, and skimmed through the article. Jason McCarthy had been sentenced to ten years in prison for rape and assault. Sophie furrowed her brow as she read. The victims were two different women, but the rape victim was never named and very few details were mentioned. The younger McCarthy had pleaded guilty to both counts in a plea deal. His father, Dennis McCarthy, had been serving as a county commissioner at the time, and his connection to the defendant had only been mentioned in the last line.

She opened the Oregon Offender Search website and keyed in *Jason McCarthy*. Two inmates came up, one serving at Deer Ridge and the other at Two Rivers. Sophie clicked the link to the one at Deer Ridge, assuming a rapist wouldn't be housed at a minimum-security facility. The man's image loaded, and even his short prison haircut and unsmiling face couldn't hide his good looks. With his time shortened by good behavior, he would be out in less than a year—before the election. She wondered what he thought of his father's run for the presidency and his political position on crime.

On impulse, she backtracked to the main website and filled out a visitation form. She could also use the trip as basic research into Oregon prisons. Maybe do a little sightseeing along the way. She'd moved to Eugene to attend the university, then went to work for the newspaper in her senior year. Her job had kept her so busy she hadn't bothered to see the rest of the state. Which was rumored to be quite beautiful.

She wondered briefly about McCarthy's other son, the law enforcement officer. Would he consent to an interview? She laughed out loud at the ridiculousness of the thought. She couldn't even get Jackson to talk to her half the time— and they were friends now. Sort of. But she would still search for the second son's name and call his place of employment. You couldn't win if you didn't play.

Chapter 17

Jackson drove out Sixth Avenue toward the Texan Motel, relishing the extended daylight and still hoping to get home before Benjie's bedtime. He might have to go back to work afterward, but he tried not to miss both dinner and bedtime with the boy. He sometimes wondered if his absence had been more of a problem for Katie in her younger years than he'd realized. A familiar guilt washed over him. Renee, his ex, may have been responsible for Katie's drinking, but it was his fault Katie no longer had a mother. He was trying not to make any mistakes with Benjie. The boy's biological father was a sociopath, and Jackson worried that no amount of *nurture* could change the *nature* Benjie had been born with. Jackson shook off the worry. So far, his adopted son was the sweetest kid he'd ever been around.

He pulled into the motel and parked in front of the office, knowing his presence might be temporarily bad for their business. But if he didn't get some cooperation, he would make sure patrol units gave them and their often-sleazy customers extra attention. He checked his phone for the time: *6:55.* The motel clerk he wanted to see should be starting her shift any minute. Jackson went inside, pleased to see the older woman behind the counter. A second clerk, a heavyset guy with a man-bun, was talking to her about a customer. They both looked up, and the woman made a groaning sound.

Her attitude irritated him and he didn't try to hide it. "One of your customers was murdered and I need your help. Either get on board or I'll have patrol officers and journalists crawling all over this place. The junkies and hookers will scatter like cockroaches, and you may not get their business back."

"There's no need to get nasty." She crossed her arms and gave him a look.

Jackson took out his phone, opened the image Jasmine had sent, and held it out. "The victim had one of your room-key cards, so we know she stayed here."

Silence.

He locked eyes on the woman. "What's your name?" He needed her surname and to see if she would be truthful.

A pause. "Betty Marsdale." She took off her sweatshirt and nodded at the other clerk.

He grabbed his thermos and started to leave.

"Not yet." Jackson shifted his weight and became suddenly aware that the carpet smelled like the inside of a sweaty shoe. He never got immune to such things. He scrolled to the victim's image and held out his phone to the male clerk.

"Is she dead?" The guy looked upset.

"Yes, murdered. I just said that."

"Uh, right. Sorry. But no, I've never seen her."

Jackson turned to Marsdale. "You said this woman looked familiar. I need you to find her name." He turned the photo so the older clerk could see it, but she didn't bother to look.

"I think she checked in Saturday before my shift. But I saw her leave Sunday night."

Progress! But it would have been nice to know that already. "Why didn't you tell me that last night?"

"I didn't remember until later."

Jackson let it go. "What time did she leave?"

"I'm not sure. Ten-thirty?"

"Was she alone?"

"Yes."

"Was she carrying anything?"

"I don't think so."

"Did you notice anything else? Like her mood? Did she seem happy? Or worried?"

"Whoa. I barely remember seeing her." Marsdale logged into the motel's computer. "I'll see if I can find her registration."

The male clerk, edging toward the door, asked, "Can I leave now?"

"No. You need to stay and handle the business for a few minutes. Betty is busy." The last thing he needed was for his witness to get distracted by a customer.

The clerk sighed, put down his thermos, and started texting someone.

Marsdale spent another minute searching, then said, "Cam Le."

Finally! He'd hated calling her Jane Doe. "Spell that for me, please."

The woman rushed through it. "Just one E."

Jackson made a note. "What time did she check in?"

"Saturday at five-thirty."

"Did she have a car? If so, where is it?"

"There's no license plate on file." Marsdale stepped away from the computer. "Can I get to work now?"

Jackson ignored her request. "Where are the woman's things? Her luggage?"

Marsdale shrugged and glanced at the other clerk.

His eyes went wide. "Don't look at me. I don't clean or even check the rooms."

Jackson wanted to slap them both. "Who does? And what room was Cam Le in?"

"The maid does the rooms. Her name's Elena, and she works from nine to three."

Crap! Frustration made him bite the inside of his cheek. "Show me the room Cam Le stayed in. Then show me where you keep lost-and-found items."

Marsdale gave Jackson a sideways look. "The room is empty now, but we had guests in there last night. So I don't know what you expect to find."

"Just show me." He wasn't sure what he hoped to accomplish, but he had to check it out. It was the last place the victim had been. What if she'd left something in the closet? Or there were bloodstains? Maybe Cam Le had been involved in something criminal. Most of the homicide victims he'd investigated lately had been frauds or liars.

Jackson turned to the male clerk. "Thanks for staying." He nodded at Marsdale. "Let's go."

She grabbed a master key card from a drawer and headed out the front door. Jackson followed her to the end of the building, and they went inside room number seven. The carpet smelled just as bad as the front lobby's, and the once-white curtains were stained with cigarette smoke. The no-frills space held a bed, a sturdy plastic chair, and a small, beat-up table. No closets or drawers. The bathroom was just as minimalist. Disappointed, Jackson searched anyway, checking the walls and carpet for bloodstains. He heard the clerk sighing as she waited. Too bad. She was on the clock and getting paid.

He looked into the small trashcan, but it had a fresh

plastic bag. Jackson lifted it out and checked underneath. Nothing but stains. He examined the bathroom sink and tub, which were surprisingly free of stray hairs. After ten minutes, he turned to the clerk. "Let's check the laundry room and wherever you keep left-behind items."

"I think you're wasting your time." Marsdale headed back out, locking the door after they exited. "Mostly what gets left behind here are syringes and used condoms."

Jackson didn't let the image linger in his mind.

In the front office, they went behind the counter and passed through an interior door. The back room was long and narrow and divided into sections. The front area functioned as a break room with a couch and a couple of employee lockers. The next section served as a large supply closet, stuffed with toilet paper, plastic bags, and cleaning supplies. The far end held two industrial-sized washing machines and matching dryers.

The clerk approached a counter in the supply area. "If the maid found anything, it would be here," she said.

The empty space made Jackson clench his teeth. What had happened to the poor woman's stuff? He took the victim's key from his satchel and held it out for Marsdale. "Do you recognize this key? Does the motel have guest lockers?"

The clerk laughed. "We only have two employee lockers, and no one even locks them."

"What's your policy for items left in the room?"

"We hold them for twenty-four hours." The clerk pointed at the small empty counter. "Then throw them away. But that doesn't happen often."

Something was wrong. Everything he'd learned pointed to the idea that Cam Le had recently arrived in the country. Most likely she had at least one piece of luggage. "Does anyone ever take stuff home? I mean, if it has value?" He tried to make it sound acceptable. "Which would make more sense than throwing it in the trash."

A long silence while the clerk stared at her hands. Finally she looked up and said, "I'll call Elena."

"Tell her she's not in trouble. I just need to see the dead woman's possessions. Particularly her phone."

Marsdale made the call, then carried on an intense conversation in Spanish that Jackson didn't understand. When it was over, she looked sheepish. "Elena says there was only a small carry-on with some clothes and a few personal items. She donated those to St. Vincent and gave the luggage to her son. But she swears there was no phone."

What the hell? His frustration felt like heat in his chest, and for a moment, Jackson didn't dare speak. "Call her back and tell her to round up everything that belonged to Cam Le and bring it to the police department. Right now." He knew the process would likely be pointless. But the victim's key had been important to her, and obviously it unlocked something. Maybe the suitcase had a compartment . . . and maybe the maid's son hadn't discovered it. Jackson shook his head. Wishful thinking. The burn in his chest morphed into anguish—that a murder victim's belongings had been treated so carelessly.

"Hey, don't look so upset." The motel clerk walked over to the cabinet with the employee lockers and opened one. "Elena found the woman's passport and stashed it. Just in case she showed back up."

Chapter 18

Evans grabbed Schak's arm as he headed out. "Hey, wait. Do you have Shaffer's phone?"

Schak set his satchel down on the conference table and scrounged through it. "I had only spent a few minutes with the device before you called me about Griffen's interrogation. But I think the person to contact is her sister, Carene Zindler, spelled with a C and located in Eugene."

Evans keyed the name into the notes file in her own phone. "Did you find a tablet or computer?"

"A laptop. But it needed a password so I turned it over to the tech people." Schak handed her a plastic evidence bag. "Fortunately, her emails are on this phone."

"Great." Evans needed him to return to the victim's home, but she hesitated. Technically, she was running this case, but Schak had seniority and it felt strange to give him directions.

He spared her the decision. "I'll head back out to the scene. There's more to search and collect." He grinned. "If that's okay with you, boss."

"I'll meet you there after I've talked to the sister." Evans pulled the victim's phone from the bag. "Unless she gives me a lead I need to follow. But I'll keep you updated. And you let me know if you find anything I can use with the sister."

"Will do." Schak gave her a mock salute and hustled out.

Evans clicked the Facebook icon on the screen and was automatically logged into Shaffer's account. She keyed the sister's name into the search bar and waited for her page to load. The woman had posted just twenty minutes earlier: *Headed to Mac's to dance. Blues jam!*

Mac's? Was that the nightclub in the Vet's building? Evans used her own phone to google the business. Yep. Located on Willamette. Oh boy, another bar scene. She studied Zindler's image. Thirty-five or so, with shoulder-length blondish hair. A narrow face, much like her sister's, but not as pretty for some indefinable reason. Now, if she could just find the woman in a crowded cocktail bar.

The Veteran's Club was a massive white-brick structure with a colonial look. The nightclub inside was run by someone else now, but the vets still leased out the big ballrooms for events like weddings and anniversaries. As Evans entered the big double doors, the music hit her. Loud, sloppy southern blues. She preferred techno and funk, but at least this sound was danceable. She made her way back to the club, a dark L-shaped space with a dozen guitars mounted on the walls. At the end of the counter, she tried to get a bartender's attention.

Finally, a tall man in a baseball cap walked over. "What can I get you?"

"I need to locate this woman." She showed him the sister's Facebook image.

He smiled. "Carene is always dancing."

Evans pushed through the crowd, not surprised that nearly everyone was over fifty. At the edge of the packed dance floor, she spotted the woman, twirling with an older man. Evans braced herself. Notifying next-of-kin was the worst part of their job, and Jackson usually had to do it. But now that Lammers was assigning her homicides and not just assaults, she would have to bear that responsibility. Evans slipped sideways through the dancers and grabbed Zindler's arm. "Excuse me!" She shouted to be heard.

The woman looked annoyed at first, then worried. She stepped close. "What's this about?"

"I'm Detective Evans. Let's go somewhere quiet to talk."

The sister started to say something, then stopped and headed for a pair of swinging doors at the side. Evans followed her into a hallway that lead back to the main lobby. Zindler took a seat on the carpeted stairs. "Is this about Jola?"

"Yes." Evans eased down next to her. "I'm sorry to bring you bad news." She paused to let the woman brace herself. "A co-worker found Jola unresponsive in her bed this morning. She's dead."

Zindler gasped, then pulled in a gulp of air. For a moment, she was silent. Finally, she exhaled and let out a sob at the same time. "I worried this would happen."

This? "What specifically were you concerned about?"

"That Jola would drink too much. Or take too many pills. Or both." The grieving sister looked up. "I assume that's how she died?"

"It looks like that on the surface, but we're investigating all possibilities."

The sister burst into tears and sobbed for several minutes. Evans paced the lobby while she waited. A couple came through the door and looked them both over as they passed. Evans wished they had someplace more private, but she wanted to find out what she could and get back to work. She knew she had to consider Zindler a suspect, but her instinct was to override that. When the sister was calm again, Evans sat back down. "I have to ask some important questions."

"Okay."

"When was the last time you saw Jola?"

"A week ago. She met me here and hung out for a while. I was trying to cheer her up."

"She's been depressed?" The co-worker had mentioned that too.

She nodded. "At first it was just the divorce, then Jola started having PTSD from a sexual assault that happened years ago." Zindler struggled to control her emotions. "She started seeing a counselor, but I guess it was too little, too late."

"What's the counselor's name?" Evans pulled her phone and opened her note app.

The woman pulled a tissue from a tiny strap-purse and blew her nose. "I can't remember at the moment."

Time to get the uncomfortable question over with. "Where were you last night?"

Zindler seemed confused. "What do you mean?"

"It's just a general question about what you did last evening, say between eight and midnight."

"I had dinner with a friend and got home around eight. Then I called Mom, and we talked about Jola and how to help her." Tears ran down Zindler's cheeks. "I should have called Jola instead."

The man she'd been dancing with came into the lobby, looking concerned.

"Give us five more minutes," Evans said, relieved that the grieving sister had someone to lean on. She turned back to Zindler. "When was the last time you talked to Jola?"

"Technically, last week when we were here. But I texted her Friday and asked if she wanted to see a movie with me. She said she wasn't feeling well." The woman shook her head.

"I knew it was bullshit. She just didn't want to go out."

Evans planned to check the victim's text messages to verify all that. But she was inclined to believe the sister. Griffen, on the other hand, was a viable suspect. "Did you know Jola and her ex-husband were having a dispute about their dog?"

"Oh yeah. Another reason my sister was upset. That jackass could've just let her have Scooter, but no. He had to be a dick about it."

"You don't like Jeff Griffen?"

Zindler choked out a bitter laugh. "No one does. I don't know how Jola ever got involved with him. He must be really good in bed." She laughed again. "Or maybe just really charming when he needs to be."

"Has Griffen ever been violent with her?"

The woman gasped. "Was Jola attacked? Did he kill her and take the dog?"

So the sister thought it was possible too. Evans decided to pick up Griffen again. They could bring him in for questioning as many times as necessary. "Jola has no obvious signs of trauma, but we'll know more after the autopsy."

"What about Scooter? Is he in the house with Jola's body?" The sister burst into tears again.

"Griffen came to the house and took the dog last night."

"Fucker." Zindler sucked in a deep breath, then stood. "I'm gonna get her dog back."

Chapter 19

Evans entered her side of the duplex, locked the door, and set her shoulder bag on the counter. The place looked smaller every time she came home. And she could hear her neighbor's TV again. The idiot never muted the commercials. It was time to buy a real house. She finally had enough equity and cash saved to pull off an upgrade. Maybe even a home in the hills instead of the flatlands.

But right now, she needed to burn off stress. On the way to her bedroom, she pulled off her jacket and weapon, relieved to be done with formal attire for the day. She changed into workout clothes, tucked her house key into a pocket, and headed back out. Her first thought was to make it a short run. But she always told herself that—just to get past the initial half-mile.

Soon after, she settled into a pace and let her mind roam. She tried to think about Todd and what she would do on her days off, but she kept coming back to her current case. She needed something more solid on the victim's ex. The neighbor who overheard the argument about the dog wasn't all that viable now that Griffen had admitted to being there. They needed a witness to place him at the home later in the evening, around Shaffer's time of death. Evans still had to check out phone and email messages, but she would do that when she got back to the house.

After a shower, Evans grabbed a beer from the fridge and settled into her comfortable chair. She turned on the victim's phone and checked the log. Only one call had come in the day of Shaffer's death, and the ID was marked *Dentist*. She'd received four texts though. Evans scrolled through them. The first was from the same dentist, reminding her of a scheduled appointment that week, and the second text had been sent by her carpool co-worker and simply said: *Here.* Shaffer's mother had sent a collection of happy emojies, and the last message had come from Griffen. Her ex had messaged: *We need to talk. I'll come by later.*

None of it was any help. She needed threats and conflict, communication the DA could show a jury to prove hostility. Evans scrolled through the previous day's messages, skimming a long text exchange between Shaffer and her sister about a hike they'd been planning together that Shaffer kept putting off. Her sister seemed both irritated and worried. Further back, Evans found a text from someone labeled Nancy/Counselor, who had also reminded her about an appointment. Evans wondered if Shaffer had shown up. She used her own phone to call the number and got a message: "This is Mid-Valley Counseling Services. If you're feeling suicidal, please call the National Suicide Prevention Lifeline at 1-800-273-8255. For all other concerns, please leave a message and we'll get back to you as soon as we can."

Evans picked up her computer tablet and searched for the counseling website. Once she found it, she clicked on the staff's dropdown menu and found *Nancy Kenneth*. A small success—if the counselor would actually talk to her. She would call her tomorrow. Evans searched the phone again, this time looking for emails. She only found a few, and most were spam. The victim's work email might be more productive. She added *New Leaf* to her list of tasks for the next day.

Evans' phone beeped in her hand. A text from Todd: *Can I come over? I know you're working a case, but we could both use some R&R.*

Evans smiled. This was a booty call, but why not? She wouldn't let him stay long—because it wasn't that kind of relationship—but taking a personal break was called for. She got up and changed out of her PJs into a sexy sleeveless dress and opened another bottle of beer.

Chapter 20

Wednesday, July 10, 3:15 a.m.

Jackson woke to the sound of Benjie's soft whimpering again. He waited a minute, hoping the boy would settle back down. But his cries grew louder, so Jackson pushed himself to get up. His back ached, and he struggled to read the digital time on the clock across the room. It didn't matter anyway. Jackson padded down the hall and into the boy's room. Benjie's eyes were open, but Jackson knew he was still asleep and having bad dreams. He lay next to the boy in his narrow bed, stroked his hair, and whispered comforting things.

A hand gently touched his shoulder, and Kera whispered, "I can do this. You need what little sleep you get."

Jackson rolled to face her, noticing how her thin sleep shirt showed off her breasts and long legs. "Thanks," he whispered, his voice catching. "But I'm okay. He's settling down."

"Go back to sleep. You have to get up in two hours." Kera sat on the edge of the bed and nudged him. "I can always nap later when the boys do."

Jackson gave in to her big heart and sat up. He put his arm around her and kissed her forehead. "Thank you." He hurried away before she could see how aroused he was.

Back in bed, he lay there, unable to sleep. His thoughts bounced from thinking about his murder case to thinking about how much he wanted Kera. Just as he was finally drifting off, he felt her slide into his bed. He assumed she had Benjie with her, so he didn't move or open his eyes. A moment later, she pressed herself against his backside and whispered, "I've missed you."

Three hours later, he sat down at his desk, the building quiet and empty around him. He wasn't contractually obligated to start work early, but he felt compelled to. The victim's family still had no idea what had happened, and he was no closer to solving her homicide. But at least he had her passport now and knew Cam Le had been born in Viet Nam forty-three years earlier. The date had surprised him; she looked much younger. But now he understood her spina bifida. During the war, the US military had blanketed Viet Nam in Agent Orange, causing a generation of miscarriages and birth defects. But the poor woman hadn't filled out the Personal Data and Emergency Contact section of her passport, so he still had no idea who her next-of-kin was. But he'd notified the department's public liaison, in case someone called to ask about Ms. Le.

His strategy now was to call international airlines, hoping to find some information. A contact person or address—a detail that might lead him to her family or an understanding of why she'd come to Eugene, Oregon. Most foreign tourists visited New York or L.A., sometimes the Grand Canyon. So he suspected she knew someone here. Or maybe had landed a job.

He googled the phrase *flights from Viet Nam to USA* as a starting point. Two travel-search sites came up, followed by Philippine Airlines. He clicked the airline link, found a contact number, and made the call. *Probably the first of many,* he thought. He expected to waste half his day on hold while they tracked down someone who spoke English. Jackson sighed and sipped coffee while the line rang.

The customer-service person who picked up spoke English fairly well, and Jackson felt a surge of hope. He introduced himself and asked to speak to a supervisor.

"I can help you," the young man insisted cheerfully. "Please."

"I need information about a murder victim. Her name is Cam Le, and she arrived in Eugene, Oregon a few days ago. Her passport indicates she flew here from Viet Nam." So much speculation. She could be a local resident who traveled regularly.

"I'm sorry for her," the man said. "And I'd like to assist. But Cam Le is a very common name." He sounded amused. "What are her other names? And her birthdate?"

Jackson glanced at the second line on the passport. "Cam Hoa Thi. Should I spell them?"

"No, just tell me the birthdate."

Jackson gave him the information and was abruptly put on hold with pop music.

The wait was surprisingly short. The customer-service guy came back on and reported, "Cam Hoa Thi Le provided an emergency contact name and phone number when she purchased her ticket."

Yes! He was finally making progress.

"Are you ready for the information?"

"Of course."

The man rattled off names Jackson didn't recognize. "Would you spell all that, please?"

"N-G-U-Y-E-N. That's the family name." The man paused. "L-I-N-H and H-U-E. They mean spiritual lily flower."

"Thanks." He understood that in her home country, the

family name would be given first, so he wrote it that way. He jotted down the phone number, then asked, "Anything else?"

"I have the customer's address too."

Jackson struggled with how to format the information and asked the service representative to send him an email with all the details. He thanked the man and clicked off, eager to move on with his task.

No one answered his call to the emergency contact, so he left a brief message, not mentioning that Cam Le was dead. He would eventually if the person ever returned his call. As he ended the call, he realized the contact person might not speak English. He hoped she would recognize her friend's name and call anyway. If not, he would call the Asian association and ask for their help.

Evans poked her head into his cube. "Any update on your case?"

"Sort of. The motel had her passport, and the airline gave me contact information. I called, but it's probably the middle of the night in Viet Nam, so no answer." Jackson sipped his now-cold coffee. "What about your case?"

Evans came in and sat down. "I'm pretty sure it's a domestic. The victim had filed for divorce and kept the dog. The husband admits to fighting with her about the dog an hour or so before she died."

"What's the cause of death?"

"Either overdose or asphyxiation. The autopsy is this afternoon."

"Have you interrogated the ex?"

"We did. And he lawyered up. But I'm headed out to question neighbors. We need another witness to nail this guy."

"Good luck."

"You too." Evans patted his knee and walked out.

Her touch had little effect this time. Kera's visit to his bed earlier had been the physical and emotional salve he'd needed. Jackson checked his to-do list, then trotted down to the front desk to see if the motel maid had dropped off the victim's suitcase. He worried he would have to go out and round it up. The idea irritated him, especially since he also expected to find the suitcase empty. But he had to locate it and examine it. A thorough investigation called for it.

The officer at the plexiglas window checked her visitor log and shook her head. "Sorry, but no."

Jackson stepped into the hall and called the motel. A male voice answered—the clerk from the night before who'd been headed home. "Jackson again. Is your maid, Elena, on duty?"

"She just got here. Why?"

"I need to talk to her."

"She doesn't speak much English."

Crap! "I need the suitcase she took home and I need it now. Go tell her."

"Uh, I don't speak much Spanish."

The burn was back in his chest. "How do you communicate?" Before the clerk could respond, Jackson snapped, "I'm headed there now. Get Betty on the line and tell her to meet me." He was so frustrated he couldn't remember the older clerk's last name. But she'd spoken Spanish to Elena and he needed a translator.

"Betty doesn't answer her phone on her days off."

Jackson bit back a response and took a deep breath. "I'll be there shortly." He clicked off and stepped back to the front desk. "Please locate a patrol officer who speaks Spanish and have him or her meet me at the Texan Motel ASAP."

"Yes, sir."

Jackson hustled upstairs, grabbed his shoulder bag, and

headed out. He'd never spent so much time just trying to identify a victim and track down personal information. As he climbed into his vehicle, he realized that wasn't quite true. An excavation crew had once found a skeleton hanging from a tree, and after months of effort, his team had finally given up their search for his ID. The man had likely committed suicide a decade earlier.

Thirty minutes later, with Officer Marino's assistance, Jackson finally learned that the maid's son who had the luggage was working a construction job in Portland, where he made better wages, and would be home Friday night. Jackson resisted the urge to lecture the nervous cleaning woman. He asked for her son's number, made the call, and had to leave a message. He handed the phone to Marino and asked him to repeat it in Spanish just to cover the bases.

Jackson left the motel, lips pressed tightly together. He would interrogate Buck Hinsic at the jail while he gave Andres Garcia time to get back to him. If the son didn't bother, Jackson would have to make the dreaded two-hour drive to Portland.

Chapter 21

Evans drove south on Willamette, feeling overwhelmed by everything she and Schak had to investigate on their own. Electronics, bank records, and witnesses. But since they had a viable suspect, they were focused on him. Schak was digging through the victim's laptop files—accessed by the tech team—to look for threatening messages and whatever else popped up. She hoped to find another neighbor who had witnessed the couple's argument or could pinpoint when Griffen had left his ex-wife's house on the night of her death. Which could still turn out to be a suicide. Hopefully, the pathologist would be able to determine the cause this afternoon.

Mid-Valley Counseling was on her way though, so it would be her first task of the day. Evans slowed and started looking for addresses on the cluster of new medical buildings. She pulled into the last structure, then buttoned her jacket as she hurried inside. Summer mornings in Eugene were always cooler than she expected.

At the counter, she introduced herself and asked to speak with Nancy Kenneth.

The receptionist, who looked like an oversized fifteen-year-old, seemed confused by the request. "Do you have an appointment? I don't see your name on her schedule."

"I'm investigating the death of one of her clients. Please let Ms. Kenneth know I'm here."

The girl blinked, then picked up the desk phone. Evans felt movement behind her and turned to see a middle-aged woman in sweatpants get up from a waiting chair and bolt from the lobby.

The receptionist's mouth dropped open and she stared at the retreating client.

Evans shrugged. "I guess she changed her mind. Nancy Kenneth, please."

It took a few more minutes, but she eventually walked into a small office in the corner. The view out the window featured the side of the medical building next door. *Ugh.* The counselor was harder to pin down. Short silver hair, lean frame, big glasses, and a black button-up shirt. She could have been forty. Or sixty. Male or female. But with the name Nancy, Evans assumed the correct pronoun was *she*.

The receptionist tried to introduce Evans but couldn't remember her name, then walked away in embarrassment. The poor girl was probably somebody's daughter, and they kept her employed out of pity.

Evans shook Kenneth's hand, stated her name and business, and sat down. "I only need a few minutes of your time."

"I really can't talk about a client."

"She's dead. And I need to know why. Please don't make me get a subpoena."

A long silence.

"I'm so sorry to hear about her passing," the counselor finally said. "What do you want to know?"

"Did Jola talk about suicide?"

"Sometimes."

"How recently? And what did she say?"

"Jola felt like a failure because her marriage was ending

125

and she'd been denied a promotion." Kenneth's face was expressionless, and her mouth barely moved. "And she was depressed about the state of the country. Most of my clients are."

"Did you ever think she was serious about suicide?"

"I take all such thoughts seriously. I recommended she see her primary care physician for an antidepressant, and we talked about coping strategies."

"Did she get the prescription?"

"I don't think so. She didn't want to take an SSRI."

Evans didn't blame her. "Did Jola seem to be getting worse? Were you worried?"

"She was up and down. Yes, I was concerned about her, but not in an escalating way."

No help so far.

The counselor shifted, started to speak, then stopped.

"What is it?" Evans prodded.

"Jola was dealing with a sexual assault from the past that had resurfaced. She was drunk when it happened and knew her attacker, so she had unresolved issues of guilt, shame, and anger."

Another possible motive for suicide. "Did she report it? And get justice?"

"Yes and no."

Slap on the wrist probably for the rapist. "What was she saying?"

"Just that she was having nightmares about it again. But I don't think she felt suicidal about the issue."

Evans decided to let it go and focus on their suspect. "Did Jola talk about her ex?"

"Of course. She was terribly conflicted. She loved him and hated him at the same time."

Evans didn't know what that felt like. "Did he abuse or threaten her?"

"Jeff never hit her that I know of, but he constantly undermined her self-confidence." The counselor's expression finally gave way to a hint of disgust. "And he spent all his money on himself and made her pay the bills."

Good reason to kick him out. But she needed motive for murder. "Did Jeff have any reason to kill her? Based on your conversations with Jola?"

A hesitation, as Kenneth measured her words. "I know they were in a dispute about their pet dog. But Jola never indicated she feared Jeff."

"What about money? Did Jola have resources that Jeff wanted? Will he benefit financially from her death?" When women died young, it was almost always about money or sex.

"Not that I know of." The counselor locked eyes with Evans. "How did Jola die?"

"I'll know more after the autopsy, but she wasn't physically assaulted." Had she said too much? Evans mentally backtracked. *Everyone was a suspect!* "Did you know Jola outside of this office?"

Kenneth looked startled. "Of course not. Why?"

"Just checking all the possibilities."

The counselor abruptly stood. "That's all the time I have. My first client will be here soon."

Evans decided to move along. She could subpoena Shaffer's mental health file, including the counselor's notes, if she needed to. But first, she had to learn the official cause of death. As guilty as Jeff Griffen looked, she knew the facts of the case pointed more to suicide or accidental overdose than murder.

On the drive out to the victim's neighborhood, the sky

clouded over and a light drizzle hit her windshield. Evans swore out loud. Questioning neighbors was tedious enough without getting wet. She pulled into the driveway of Shaffer's home, stared at the garage door, and wondered where the victim's car was. *Oh hell.* She'd been so focused on the ex-husband and the couple's fight she'd missed a few investigative steps. *But damn.* She also didn't have a full team. Evans texted Schak: *Does vic have vehicle?*

Evans bet herself that he would either call or text back with a one- or two-word answer. Schak hated texting—because he had stubby fingers *and* resisted change—but he'd come to realize it made sense for brief communications. And someone, likely his poor wife, had taught him how to use the voice-to-text function.

After waiting a moment, Evans grabbed a rain poncho from the backseat and climbed out. Patrol officers had questioned neighbors the night before—that's how Schak had learned about the argument—but the report submitted listed two addresses where no one had been home. Evans checked her notes, visually located the first house, and crossed the street. As she walked up the driveway past an old Explorer, her phone pinged. Schak had texted: *No car three bikes.*

Evans smiled. The old guy was coming along.

She reached the door and pounded hard—in case the occupant worked nights and was sleeping—but got no response. She knocked again even louder, shouted a few times, then finally tucked her business card into the doorframe. Walking away, she made a mental note to find the owner and try calling.

"Hey! What do you want?" The angry voice came from behind her.

Evans turned back. A man in his forties with a heavy beard stood in the doorway.

"I'm Detective Evans. I just need a few minutes of your time."

The man groaned, reached into his sweatpants, and scratched his balls.

Evans tried not to write him off. "What's your name?"

"Shawn Adams. Why?"

She bounced back to her first assessment. Men named Shawn or Travis were always trouble. "Your neighbor across the street is dead, and I need your help."

"Jola?"

"Yes. Do you know her?"

"Sort of. She's been more friendly since her husband moved out."

Evans stepped onto the covered patio to get out of the drizzle.

"But dead?" The man scratched his head this time. "That's too bad. What happened?"

"We're not sure yet. Where were you Monday evening? Say, from eight p.m. to midnight?"

He scowled. "I was here until eleven-thirty-five. That's when I leave for my midnight shift at Arco."

Crap job and crap shift. Evans had a moment of empathy. "I'm sorry to disturb your sleep."

"Huh. Can we wrap this up?"

"Did you see or hear anything unusual between Jola and her ex that night?"

"Oh yeah. They were fighting about the dog again."

"Did you hear any threats?"

"No, just a lot of back and forth about who needed the dog more."

"Did you see them? Were they inside or outside?"

"Both. He was on the front step, and she was inside the house with the door open."

"For how long?"

"I don't know. I had to eat and shower and get ready for work."

"Did you see Jeff Griffen leave?"

"I think so. A car took off around the same time I did."

A tingle ran up Evans' spine. That matched the victim's time of death—and contradicted Griffen's claim. "Describe it please."

"I'm pretty sure it was their car. A newer off-road vehicle, you know, like a Jeep." The witness shook his head. "I wish I could afford one."

"What color?"

He shrugged. "It was too dark to tell, but if I had to guess, I'd say white or silver."

Something he'd said suddenly registered. "What do you mean by *their car*?"

"They only had the one. When Jeff moved out, he took it. But he loaned it to Jola to grocery-shop."

"Sounds like you knew them fairly well."

Adams shook his head. "Not really. But they live across the street. I can't help but see and notice things."

"Did you notice the driver of the car that left around the same time you did?"

"It was definitely a man, and I just assumed it was Jeff. Jola rarely had any other visitors except a few biking friends." He shrugged. "But I sleep during the day and work at night, so I can only account for evenings and weekends."

Evans wished he'd definitively identified the driver, but she would tell Griffen that he had and see how the suspect reacted. That meant picking him up again—which she intended to do as many times as necessary. She picked her business card from the porch where it had fallen and handed it to Adams. "Call me if you think of anything important."

He took the card and used it to scratch his forehead. "Did Jeff kill her over the damn dog?"

"We don't know yet. Thanks for your time." Evans walked away, eager to find Griffen again.

But first she wanted to check the crime-scene house and see if Griffen had taken the dog's leash and things. The light rain was still coming down so she jogged across the street and up the driveway, noticing the front door was crossed with crime-scene tape. The techs had done that to keep out friends or family who might stop by. Evans walked around to the back door, where Schak had left the key under the mat.

But the door wasn't locked. Surprised, she pushed it open and stuck her head inside. Instinctively, she knew something was wrong. Kitchen drawers were open, and two floor vases had been turned over. Sometimes cops were careless when they searched a house, but not Schak. And not a victim's home. Evans backed out and reached for her phone to call him. The device rang in her hand.

"Hey. I was just going to contact you." Evans turned on her earpiece and slipped her phone and the house key into her jacket pocket. "I'm at Shaffer's place, and it looks a bit ransacked." She hadn't moved, afraid to miss or contaminate evidence.

"What do you mean? I might have left some interior doors open, but you know I'm careful."

"Did you turn over floor vases?"

"And leave them that way? No. Neither did the officer who helped me search."

"Then someone else has been here. The back door was unlocked too."

"I left it locked."

A pause while they both considered the possibilities.

"Griffen probably has a key," Evans said. "I wonder what he was looking for."

"I might know." Shack's voice was tight. "I've been reading through an envelope full of receipts I took from the house. And Shaffer withdrew fifteen hundred in cash three days ago."

Chapter 22

Jackson climbed the wide stairs to the jail's reception lobby, dreading the task at hand. He hated this building with its lack of windows and uncomfortable chairs. He'd spent more than his share of time in the processing area, booking suspects into custody. Now he was here for an interrogation he'd scheduled earlier that morning. The jail and its inmates had routines, and he couldn't afford to waste time waiting around.

The deputy behind the plexiglas greeted him by name. He didn't remember hers, so he smiled instead. "I'm here to see Buck Hinsic."

"That's right. I'll have someone bring him up."

She made a call, stashed his weapon and satchel in a vault, then escorted Jackson into the bowels of the dark maze. After the deputy unlocked a narrow side door, Jackson hesitated before entering. This space was even smaller than the interrogation rooms at the department. It had also been painted pink back when jailers believed the color could calm inmates. But now it was a weird gray and smelled moldy. "Hurry, please," he said to the departing woman. "I have a busy schedule."

Sometimes it took ten minutes for a deputy to locate and bring in an inmate, but he'd called ahead so Hinsic arrived quickly, escorted by a male deputy. The inmate wore dark-green jail scrubs, had a shaved head, and sported both ink and handcuffs on his forearms. Jackson stared at the tattoos.

One was a blocky swastika, and the other a demon with fiery red eyes.

Nice messaging.

"Sit down!" the deputy barked.

The prisoner complied but announced, "This is a waste of time."

Jackson, still on his feet, turned to the deputy. "Will you stay?" He had no desire to be alone in a room with Hinsic. Especially without the comfort of his service weapon.

"Sure."

Jackson sat across the small table from the inmate, wishing he'd heard from Quince, who was showing Hinsic's image to Asian restaurant owners. "Where were you Sunday night between nine and midnight?"

The suspect shrugged. "I can't remember."

So it would be like that. Jackson didn't let his frustration show. Instead, he got right to the grit. "Your buddy Ray Frost gave you up. So you might as well come clean."

Hinsic's body tensed and his eyes blazed. "If he named me, then he's not my *buddy*." He practically spit out the word.

"We have you on video at the restaurant."

"Bullshit."

Jackson needed to use the leverage he had—without putting Pham at risk. "And we have a positive ID on your tattoos for a recent assault."

A flicker of worry. "These are too common for that to stick."

It wasn't a denial. "If you work with us to resolve the recent hate crimes, the DA will go easy on you."

"Not a chance." More spit dribbled down the man's chin.

Jackson turned to the deputy. "Call someone to bring him a napkin, please."

The deputy hesitated for a second, then radioed the request.

Jackson turned back to the inmate. "What do you have against Asians? I'd really like to know."

"They don't belong here!" His vehemence was startling.

Jackson had no doubt Hinsic had committed hate crimes. But proving it without a solid witness would be impossible. "Are others in your Homelanders group involved in the attacks or just you?"

"I have nothing to say."

"But Ray Frost did. And we have you on video. Plus the tattoo ID. You are going down for this murder. And could get life. A plea deal is your only smart option." Little of it was true, but he needed a confession.

The inmate grunted.

They sat in silence for a minute, then the door opened, and another deputy walked in. He handed Jackson a paper towel.

"Thanks. Can you stay for a moment?" In case this got ugly.

"Okay."

With a tilt of his head, Jackson gestured for the deputies to step close. They took positions on either side of the cuffed inmate. Jackson leaned toward Hinsic. "You look kind of Asian. Is that why you hate them so much?"

"Fuck you!" Hinsic lunged, but the deputies grabbed him by the shoulders and shoved him back down.

Jackson reached over and wiped the spit off the man's chin. "After we test your DNA for a match to the murder scene, maybe we'll send it to 23andMe and see who your daddy really is."

"Cocksucker!"

Jackson hurried back to the reception area, carrying the paper towel. "Get my satchel," he commanded the desk clerk. "Then find an evidence bag inside the zip pocket." On a gut level, he believed they would match Hinsic's DNA to a crime somewhere.

Chapter 23

Evans called the crime lab, got Jasmine Parker on the phone, and asked her to send a technician out to Shaffer's house.

"Right now? Why?"

"There's been a break-in, and we need to dust for fingerprints again."

"What? We haven't even processed the first batch. And we don't plan to until we get the pathologist's report. If Shaffer's death isn't a murder, it's not a priority."

Oh hell. Evans realized the autopsy was scheduled to begin soon, and she would miss it. She felt both relieved and disappointed at the same time. The procedure was a rite of passage she needed to experience. But not right now. Something weird was happening with her case, and she needed help.

So she pressured Parker. "I need a tech person to process the back-door area. I think I see new footprints, so we have to capture those too." It had rained lightly on and off since late the night before, and she could see an outline of shoe marks just inside the door.

"I'll send Joe out soon." Parker abruptly ended the call.

Evans considered her options, then squatted and took photos of the shoe marks through the open door. She jogged back around front and yanked down the yellow tape. Before entering, she reached in her shoulder bag for booties and pulled them on while standing, grateful for good balance. She put on gloves too and unlocked the door.

As she crossed the living room, she heard Schak pull up outside. Glancing around, Evans moved through the house, looking for areas of intrusion. The hall closet was open, and a collection of plastic crates and boxes had been pulled down and searched. Evans took photos of the scattered mess, which looked like a collection of mostly biking gloves and winter scarves.

In the bedroom, a few drawers had been left open, but otherwise the room seemed untouched. Yet not quite right. She noticed the top mattress was slightly off center. Had the intruder lifted it to search? Evans replicated the action but found nothing. The whole thing was baffling. But Shaffer's bank withdrawal might explain it. If Griffen—or someone else—had known Jola Shaffer had cash, they might have come here to search for it. *No harm in stealing from the dead, right*? Evans knew how criminals thought and rationalized their actions.

Schak shuffled into the room, his paper booties making an old-lady-in-slippers sound. "We've seen some weird stuff at crime scenes before, but a break-in is new."

A memory surfaced. "Except that case on Elmira Street with the drug dealer."

"Oh yeah. We caught him searching for the stash under the house."

"What if this case is about drugs?"

"I doubt it." Schak glanced around the room.

"Or some other scam. The cash withdrawal is unusual."

Schak shrugged. "Unless she planned to buy something, say on Craigslist. They would want cash."

"Good point." Evans felt herself relax a little. "But we haven't found the money."

"Maybe she spent it already. One of the bikes in the garage looks new."

Evans knew he was just laying out possibilities. "So what was the intruder looking for?"

"Anything he could steal." Schak walked around the room, glancing into drawers.

Evans had a disturbing thought. "What if one of her neighbors searched the house? Knowing she was dead, they thought they might find and confiscate items of value."

"That's what I'm checking out. But we have her laptop and phone." He turned abruptly and strode out. Evans followed him down the hall and out into the adjoining garage. The dark space was filled with gardening tools, including a wheelbarrow, plus three bicycles. One had fenders and saddlebags, and one had fat tires for off-road adventures. The third looked sleek and new.

"These bikes seem like the only other items of value I noticed, and they're obviously still here." Schak looked disappointed. "A junkie would have taken all of them."

Evans had another thought and called Jeff Griffen. While his phone rang, she looked at Schak. "Maybe the ex came here looking for something specific that belonged to him. He might feel entitled." When Griffen didn't answer by the third ring, Evans ended the effort. "Let's go get him again. The neighbor across the street says he saw a guy in a jeep like Griffen's leave here at eleven-thirty, right around the time of death." Feeling pumped up, she strode out of the garage and into the kitchen.

"Didn't the ex claim he left at nine-thirty?" Schak asked.

"Yep. And I think he lied."

They stopped in the kitchen and looked around.

Schak caught her attention. "Anything else you forgot to

tell me?"

"Sorry, it's been a busy day." Evans grimaced. "I questioned her counselor this morning. She says Shaffer was depressed and talked about suicide."

"So it's still possible *our victim*"—he used air quotes around the words—"just drank too much, then took a sleeping pill." Schak gave Evans a look. "Aren't you supposed to be at her autopsy right now?"

"This seemed more important. I'll call the pathologist for the report as soon as we're done here."

They heard someone at the front door and turned. Joe, a crime-scene tech, stepped in and put on booties.

Evans had a flash of guilt about wasting his time. But she knew she'd made the right call. They still had no idea what had happened here on the night of Shaffer's death—or who had come in and searched the empty home. But maybe they were about to find out. She turned to Schak. "Let's go harass our suspect."

Chapter 24

Evans waited for Schak in the parking lot, then they walked into Hutch's together. The two customers and two employees all turned to stare. In their suit jackets, she and Schak didn't look like the usual cyclist clientele. Evans visually searched the mechanics' area in back. Griffen wasn't at his workstation. *Damn!* She approached the short smiley woman Griffen had called 'Deb.'

"Detective Evans again. Is Jeff Griffen here today?"

The manager's expression went dark. "No. He's taking some personal time off."

Oh no. "We need his address."

"I don't feel comfortable giving it to you. Jeff is a good guy."

Until he wasn't. "His estranged wife is dead, and he was seen leaving her house right before she died. If he's innocent, he needs to explain."

A long moment while Deb struggled with her decision. Evans suppressed the urge to prompt her. They would find the suspect one way or another.

"I'll look it up," the manager finally said. "But he moved recently, and I don't know if we have his current location."

The other employee, in dark, grease-stained clothes, stepped forward. "I know where he lives."

Schak walked toward him. "Tell us."

"Jeff is staying in one of those tiny houses on his sister's property. She lives just outside of town on Bailey Hill. You know, that house on the right with the old empty pool."

Evans tried to visualize it and couldn't.

But Schak said, "I know it."

"What's the sister's name?"

"I'm not sure. I only know the place because I've biked out there to join him for a ride."

Evans handed the manager a business card. "If you hear from Griffen, tell him to turn himself in, then call me."

As she and Schak started to leave, the helpful employee called, "Wait."

They turned back.

The guy pulled out his phone. "I have him in my Find Friends app." He tapped his screen a few times, then frowned. "Uh, he's not coming up."

Not good.

"But he could be on a long ride and out of range." The mechanic shrugged.

Evans handed him a card too. "If you hear from Griffen, same thing. Tell him to come to the department, then call me."

She glanced at Schak, and they left the bike store.

"He's in the wind," Schak said, as they walked to the parking lot. "I'll put a twenty on it."

She didn't want to take the bet. "I'll be sporting and say he'll turn up in a few days when he thinks it all through."

"Let's go see if he's home."

Evans considered leaving her vehicle to ride out with Schak, then changed her mind. She didn't trust the homeless and restless populations downtown, and their destination was only a ten- or fifteen-minute drive. More important, they might have to split up to search for Griffen. "See you there."

The residence was right where the co-worker had said and easy to spot. Sitting below the road level, the abandoned pool was an eyesore. The brick home looked neglected too, but the tiny house to the side was obviously new. Evans pulled into the circular driveway, disappointed there wasn't a car. Schak parked behind her, and they both got out.

"This is a waste of time," Schak pronounced.

"Not necessarily." Evans didn't quite believe that, but her partner's pessimism was annoying. "Let's check the tiny house first."

A gravel path led to the small structure, which sat on big cinderblocks. The rectangular home was about the size of a train car, and a water tank was visible behind the unit. "They don't have county utilities hooked up," she commented.

"Probably don't have a permit either." Schak stepped up on the railroad tie that served as a porch and pounded on the door.

While they waited for a response that wasn't coming, Evans tried to peek in the windows, but curtains prevented her from seeing much.

Schak tried the knob but it was locked. And the house was quiet.

"No car and no dog," Evans noted.

"I'm calling in an ATL." Schak reached for his phone.

"Better make it statewide. He could be running."

"Will do."

Evans wanted to talk to the sister. She searched her phone contacts for the county's property tax office, then connected the call. After a recorded message played, the line went to canned music. Schak's conversation with a dispatcher played in the background too, so Evans put in her earpiece and walked toward the main house, looking for an address.

Finally a staff person came on the line. Evans gave her name and credentials, then recited the numbers she'd just spotted on the front of the garage. "That's a Bailey Hill Road address. And I need to know who owns the property."

After a long wait and more canned music, the woman came back on. "Lisa Priven. Would you like the phone number?"

"Yes, thanks." Evans keyed it into her phone, ended the first call, and pressed the connect icon for the new number. The suspect's sister didn't answer. Evans left a terse message, then searched for the woman on Facebook. In a few minutes, she knew Lisa Priven was "in a complicated relationship," loved cats, and worked at Winco. As Evans walked back toward Schak, she called the grocery store and learned that Lisa Priven wasn't on shift.

"What did you find out?" Schak searched for a spare house key above the doorframe.

"No one home, but I have the sister's name and workplace. I'll keep checking with her."

"I'm tempted to break into this little hut," Schak said with an eager grin. "It would be so easy."

"Not worth it. We'll find him. And get a search warrant."

Her phone rang, and she snatched it out of her pocket, hoping it was Priven getting right back to her. "Lara Evans here."

"It's Gunderson. You missed the autopsy."

"I know. Sorry. Schak and I are working this one alone, and our suspect is on the run."

"Well, you'd better find him. Jola Shaffer was suffocated."

Chapter 25

A few hours earlier

While Sophie waited for her work computer to boot up, she called the spokesperson at the police department. The new woman on the job was friendlier than the last, but maybe she'd been instructed to be. The police department was taking heat for a man who'd died in the back of a police car. So they needed some positive press. "Hey, it's Sophie Speranza again."

The woman gave a soft laugh. "Every morning, like clockwork."

"Any news on the Jane Doe homicide?" The photo she'd run in the paper hadn't been helpful.

"Her name is Cam Le, and we have a couple of suspects."

Sophie took notes. "What can you tell me about them?"

"Nothing really, except that they're members of a white nationalist group called Homelanders."

An important detail. "Is the murder being labeled a hate crime?"

"Not yet."

"Are the suspects in custody?"

"You'll have to call the jail. Or Detective Jackson."

Without names, the jail couldn't tell her anything. "Any new crimes I should know about?" That was the point of the daily chat.

A pause.

Finally, the spokeswoman said, "Our maintenance crew found incendiary devices on the department's property this morning."

What the hell? "You mean bombs?"

"Just refer to them as *incendiary devices*. They've been sent to the forensics lab for analysis, and that's all I can say on the subject."

"Were they a hoax?"

"No. Now I need to get back to work."

"Any other suspicious deaths?"

Another pause.

"A woman named Jola Shaffer, age 32, died in her home late Monday, and a team is investigating."

"Died how?"

"We don't know yet."

"Jackson's leading it?"

"No, Evans is. And that's all I can tell you."

"Spell her name for me, please."

"It's just like it sounds. Bye, Sophie." The PR person hung up.

Sophie gulped some tea, then called Evans and left a message asking for information. She would follow up with a text in an hour or so. For now, she had to write up the incendiary-device story and get it posted on the website, then see what she could learn on social media about Jola Shaffer.

On her lunch break, Sophie skimmed through the profile she'd written about Dennis McCarthy. The freelance piece was ready to send to the Portland paper, except for the quotes she hoped to add. She'd gotten one from a woman who'd worked for McCarthy when he was still county commissioner. The ex-employee claimed he was verbally respectful but sexist in his actions. But a single quote wasn't nearly enough. She wanted to interview McCarthy himself, as well as talk to the vet who'd served with him in Viet Nam. Part of her wanted the other man to say great things about the candidate because she thought he was likely to win, and she wanted him to be a good president. But readers wanted the juicy stuff that public people tried to hide.

Sophie put down her cold piece of quiche and called the veteran's number again. The kid at the rally had said his uncle would be reluctant to speak to her, and he'd been right. The man had ignored two messages and two texts. But this time, he picked up on the third ring. "Who the hell is this?"

"Sophie Speranza. Is this Rick Brantley?

"Why do you want to know?"

This conversation would be challenging. "I'm writing an article about Dennis McCarthy now that he's running for president, and I'd like to know about your experience with him in the Viet Nam war."

"You're a journalist?"

"Yes, but I'm doing this piece as a citizen."

"Huh. Where did you get my name?"

"From your nephew. I met him at McCarthy's rally. He was protesting."

"He's like that. A real libtard." A pause. "What do you want to know?"

Was he slurring his words? Sophie looked at the time. A little early to be drinking. "What was McCarthy like? Did you respect him? Was he an admirable soldier?"

A bitter laugh followed. "In Viet Nam, nobody was admirable. You were either a shitty person because you followed orders and killed innocent women and children. Or you were a bad soldier because you refused to obey your commander."

She'd never heard it put that way. And the knowledge sickened her. For a moment, Sophie couldn't speak.

"You still there?"

"I am. Sorry. I'm a little stunned by your assessment."

"Why do you think so many vets came back so fucked-up? I'm lucky." A pause. "Sort of."

She wanted to know Brantley's story too, but she didn't have time right now. "Tell me about McCarthy. Anything you know or saw that seems important."

"It was a long time ago."

"Still, his actions under stress tell us who is he. And he wants to lead this country."

A lengthy pause.

"He killed our commander."

What? "You mean accidentally?"

"No. It was intentional. Knifed him in the back. Near the end of the war, that happened all the time. An average of one a day, I read somewhere."

"No shit?"

Another bitter laugh. "Some men snapped and saw that as the only way to stop the killing. They rationalized a single act of violence as the right moral choice." Brantley paused and took a sip of something. "Or maybe they just hated their commanders."

Again, she felt overwhelmed. So much information to process. So much more to ask. "Did you witness McCarthy's" —she struggled for the right word—"assault on his commander?"

"Two of us did. But we never told anyone." His speech slurred even more. "We wanted the son-of-a-bitch dead too.

All we could think about was going home."

"So you admire McCarthy for his action?"

"Hell no. It was cowardly and insu ... bor ... dinate." He struggled to pronounce the slurry word. "But I was too grateful for the reprieve to rat him out. And people were dying around me every day. So I got kind of numb to it."

Sophie didn't know how she felt about the killing of the commander either. He was doing his job too. McCarthy could have rebelled in other ways. "What else can you tell me about McCarthy?"

"Lazy and arrogant." A pause while Brantley took another sip. "There's more, but I can't tell you." The man coughed, a horrible racking sound. Then the coughs turned to sobs. "Don't use my name. I'll deny ever speaking to you." He abruptly hung up.

Damn! She'd wanted to ask the name of the other soldier who'd witnessed the murder. And to hear the rest of the story. There had to be a way to find out.

Chapter 26

Jackson stopped by Quince's cubicle on his way out. "Hey, how did you do with the surveillance footage?"

Quince spun in his chair. "You mean besides going a little blind?"

"Nothing, huh?"

"No. And I showed photos of both the victim and our suspect to at least twenty people in the restaurant industry. Nobody recognized either."

"Thanks for doing the grunt work."

Quince glanced at his computer clock. "What did you come up with?"

Jackson felt like he hadn't accomplished anything, but he thought back through his day. "Using Cam Le's passport, I tracked down her recent flight and contact person but didn't actually make contact. She also had a suitcase at the motel, but the maid took it and gave it to her son."

"Well, shit. Can we pick him up?"

"He's in Portland, working on a construction site."

"And he has the suitcase with him?"

"His mother thinks so, but the guy won't return my calls."

Quince stood. "Can we get the location of the work site? I'll pay the man a visit."

Relieved, Jackson grinned. "Thank you. I've been avoiding the drive." He reached for his phone. "I'll see what I can find out." He called the Texan, and the young male clerk answered.

Jackson launched right in. "I need the address where Elena's son is working. Please call her and find out, then get right back to me. This is important."

"I think she's still here. I'll call you back in a minute."

Quince gave him a look. "You don't have the maid's number?"

"She doesn't speak English."

Quince shrugged. "I know a little Spanish from high school."

"That might come in handy."

While they waited, they sat back down and discussed the case, with Jackson trying not to complain—except for the ridiculousness of being so understaffed.

"What about our suspects?" Quince asked.

"I questioned Buck Hinsic at the jail today. Totally uncooperative."

"Will they hold him?"

"Probably not. The only charge we have is resisting arrest."

"Too bad he wasn't carrying drugs."

Jackson started to respond, but his phone rang—the same number he had just called. The motel clerk gave him the Portland cross streets for the construction site, and Jackson passed those along to Quince. "I'll keep trying to reach Garcia."

"Have you called the Portland police?"

Jackson shook his head. "Even if they went out to the site and picked up the luggage, they wouldn't drive it here."

"Can't blame them. I'll go in the morning." Quince gestured at Jackson's satchel. "Are you headed home for the night?"

"Yes, but I'll keep working."

"Should I?"

"I'm not sure what else you can do, except to keep looking for witnesses in the area of the crime."

"If you're working late, I will too." Quince stood. "After I grab some dinner with the wife."

"Keep me posted." Jackson headed out of the building.

Later at home, he sat down at the table and looked around at his family. The sweet little boys, his amazing teenage daughter, and beautiful, loving Kera. He was a lucky man. He cleared his mind of all work thoughts and interacted with each of them as they ate. Katie reported that she'd found a job busing tables, and his chest filled with pride and worry. She was a young adult now, and the money she would earn would give her the independence to move away from him. But Kera was back in his life and searching for a home to share. Benjie was his usual precocious self, one minute lecturing him about the nutritional value of vegetables and the next talking excitedly about the fun of making gak at preschool. Jackson promised to make some at home with him that weekend.

After dinner, he took his phone and case file out to the back deck to work. With both boys in the house, the noise and distractions could be overwhelming. He was relieved to know Kera was securing a bigger place for all of them. He'd loved the thought of having a home office, but they would need four bedrooms just to accommodate everyone, so he was probably wishful-thinking.

Jackson checked his to-do list. At the top was *Locate luggage!* He sighed and tried to reach Andres Garcia again, texting this time and hoping to get a reaction. Leaving voicemail had become a dead zone. Thanks to the onslaught of spam calls, nobody answered their phones or listened to messages anymore. Jackson used the voice recorder to produce his text, then had to heavily edit the screwed-up parts and add in capitals. He missed the simplicity of phone calls. In the end, his message read: *Please call or text Detective Jackson, Eugene Police. I need the suitcase your mother gave you from the motel. This is very important. You are not in trouble!*

He hit the send button and glanced at his list again. Nothing that couldn't wait until tomorrow. He went back inside and joined Kera and the boys at the table putting puzzles together. Katie soon joined them, and they switched to Uno. An hour later, as Kera announced bedtime, Jackson's phone rang in his jacket pocket. *Crap!* His gut told him the contact was work-related. Everyone at the table went quiet and looked at him.

"Excuse me." He grabbed his jacket from the back of a chair and reached for the cell as he walked away. The call was from Lammers, and she skipped the pleasantries. "The restaurant where the woman's body was found is about to burn down."

"Oh shit. Anybody hurt?"

"I don't know."

"Or apprehended?"

"Not yet. But you should get out there. Arsonists are known to admire their work."

"On my way." Jackson scrambled to make sense of the information. Maybe the fire was another escalation in the Homelanders' hate-crime spree. He strode back to the table, smiling to reassure everyone. "I'm sorry, but I have to go out to a crime scene." He focused on Kera. "It's a fire, and no one has been hurt." She usually assumed when he was called out to a crime that someone had been murdered.

Kera was a sympathetic soul. "I'm relieved." She stood and gave him a hug. "Be safe anyway."

Jackson's body hummed with pleasure. "This shouldn't take long, but I'll text if I have to stay out late."

"No you won't," Katie said, making Kera laugh.

Jackson gave them both an apologetic grin, kissed the boys goodnight, and headed out.

He drove like a cop on a mission but without the siren. He could have used it, but on a Wednesday evening, there was no need. After a few minutes, traffic stopped coming in the opposite direction altogether, indicating a roadblock ahead. Once he saw the first-responder lights in the distance, the trip out West Eleventh felt like deja vu. He'd just done the same thing two nights ago. Now the same restaurant was on fire. He hoped it was true that no one had been hurt. At this hour, the business was likely closed, but a few employees might still be in the building. It seemed reasonable to think the same perp who'd killed Cam Le in the back parking lot was responsible for the fire.

Buck Hinsic and his hateful expressions flashed in Jackson's mind. Had the thug been released on bail? And torched the Golden Dragon to get even for his arrest? Or maybe Hinsic and his group intended to show law enforcement they weren't intimidated.

Jackson tensed and gripped the wheel tighter. No matter how hard or how smart he worked, he often felt helpless to prevent crimes from happening. Picking up perps after the fact wasn't good enough. Especially if the county system just turned them loose.

As he raced toward the scene, the lights grew brighter and took on distinction. Red-and-blue flashing from patrol units, plus a steady red glow from the fire engines, and an orange intensity from the fire. The flames shot up from the building in sporadic intervals, brightening the sky and giving shape to the vehicles blocking off the street. Dread filled his gut. Arson-set fires weren't common in Eugene, and this one troubled him.

He also found it ironic that the perp had targeted a business that wasn't owned by Asians anymore. It still served Chinese food and was staffed by the same crew. But the people who would be hurt most were the Caucasian owners and the local mostly-white customers.

The car ahead turned, and Jackson spotted barriers and patrol cops diverting traffic on both sides of the street. Ignoring the officers, he drove up the middle to pass the barriers, then pulled off to the side and parked. As he climbed out of his car, a thought hit him. *What if the murderer had burned the building to destroy evidence?*

But what? They already had the security videos, which showed nothing. And the victim had been found thirty feet from the building. Had she been killed inside, then dragged out and dumped?

Feeling the blaze's heat, Jackson unbuttoned his jacket as he strode toward the fire captain, who stood next to his rig, occasionally shouting orders.

"Hello, sir. I'm Detective Jackson."

"Captain Warzog."

They shook hands, meeting officially for the first time.

"A woman was murdered behind this building three nights ago," Jackson said. "What can you tell me about the fire?"

"It's burning hot in three places, so I'm guessing we'll find fire-igniters and evidence of arson."

Jackson stared at the blaze, which had engulfed the entire structure. "Anyone suspicious hanging around?"

"No, but that hasn't been my focus. We're just trying to keep it contained, so we don't lose the businesses on either side."

A gust of wind hit the area, and the fire shifted. Two firefighters dragged their hose to the left and kept up the steady water pressure.

"Did anyone go into the building to check for civilians?"

"No, it was too late."

Dread filled Jackson's gut. If a cook or food server had been inside, this could be another murder. "I need to look around and see if anyone is lurking or watching."

The captain pointed to a small crowd of people in the Burger King parking lot next door. "We've told them to stay back, but again, not my focus." He turned and gestured across the wide main street. "There's more over there."

The wind kicked up again, and suddenly Warzog was running toward a fireman who was on the ground. Jackson started to follow, but the captain yelled for him to stay back. *Right.* He wasn't wearing protective gear, and the heat was already getting to him.

Jackson jogged left across the divider, then hugged the fast food building as he made his way toward the group of bystanders. Young people, he noted. As he approached, their profiles came into focus. Three teenage boys, a young girl, and one older man in the back. They all turned when they finally heard his footsteps.

"What are you doing here?" Jackson locked eyes on the older man. Gray-haired and thin, he didn't look like either of the Homelanders they'd picked up and interrogated.

"Uh, nothing. Just watching," a teenage boy responded.

He grabbed the girl's arm and tugged. "Let's go."

Up close, the kid now looked older. Jackson wondered if he had a warrant or a reason to avoid the police. But he let the two walk away and stepped toward the older man. "Do you live around here?"

"Sort of. We were just walking back from the store, saw the fire, and called it in."

Interesting. Perps sometimes reported their own fires. But the man had said *we.* "You're all together?"

"Yes. These are my sons."

Probably not the arsonist. "Did you see anyone around the building?"

"No. Sorry."

"You should probably move along. Wind shifts are making this fire dangerous."

The guy nodded, and the three shuffled into another parking lot. Jackson turned back and started across the street toward the larger crowd. As he gained distance from the roar of the blaze, he heard a faint chirping sound. He pulled his phone from his pocket. Lammers again. His gut tightened as he took the call. "I'm at the scene. What have you got?"

"A shooting at Lucky Noodle, where the old man was assaulted last week."

Chapter 27

Jackson bolted to his car and started to drive away. Remembering his promise, he stopped and texted both his girlfriend and his daughter, telling them he'd be working late. He hoped Lammers would call his team to help process the new crime scene.

As he raced down the still-blocked main avenue, Jackson tried to visualize who was dead. Pham, the old man? Or a Homelander? Lammers hadn't been given detailed information. But maybe Hinsic or one of his followers had gone from one restaurant to the next, starting fires. Or attempting to. The old guy lived above his business and had said he intended to buy a gun to protect himself.

Crap! Jackson wished he'd tried harder to talk him out of it. But the man had the rights to own a gun and to defend himself and his home. Still, Jackson felt guilty that the department hadn't been able to protect him. But patrol officers couldn't be everywhere, and he and his team needed evidence to put people away.

He turned on Garfield and spotted another fire engine coming his way. A patrol unit's light flashed in his rearview mirror. Dispatch had probably called a firetruck from Springfield and had brought in off-duty officers to the new incident. But at least the hunt for the suspect might be short.

Jackson parked in front of the dark building and jumped out. He seemed to be the first person on the scene. He ran to the front door. Locked. He hurried around to the back, glancing around for incendiary devices. *Oh hell.* What if a Homelander, maybe Hinsic himself, had planted the devices around the department? What if the thug had actually intended to set their building on fire? And had been interrupted? A few officers were always on duty, even in the middle of the night.

Instinctively, Jackson reached for his service weapon. This scene had not been secured.

As he rounded the back corner, he slowed and nearly ran into Pham Thi Boc, who was also pointing a gun. "Police!" Jackson shouted. "Put it down!" Training called for him to be loud.

"Don't shoot!" the old man cried. He dropped to his knees and slid his weapon to the side. A strange wailing/praying sound came from his skinny chest.

"It's okay, Boc. It's Jackson. You can get up. Just leave the weapon."

A patrol officer charged into the scene and picked up the weapon. After tucking it into a pocket, she reached for her handcuffs and said, "Turn around and put your hands behind your back."

"That's not necessary," Jackson said. "I'll get his statement. You secure the scene."

The officer tucked away the cuffs, then ran past the old man. Jackson saw her stop and kneel down. He noticed the shooting victim for the first time. His dark clothes blended with the asphalt, and the small motion-sensor lights on the back of the building didn't illuminate much.

Jackson touched the old man's arm. "Wait right here for a moment, then we'll get you inside." He jogged up to the victim, who was on his side, and asked the officer, "You checked his pulse?"

"Yes. He's dead." She stood. "Looks like two bullet wounds, one in his chest and one in his stomach."

Jackson stared at Hinsic's face and body. He'd been shot from the front. So the incident had probably been self-defense as Pham had reported. Jackson nudged the officer. "Secure the rest of the building."

"Yes, sir." She jogged to the next corner, her gun still drawn.

As Jackson moved back toward Pham, another patrol cop hustled around the corner. "Watch the body," Jackson instructed him. He touched the old man's arm. "Let's go sit inside."

Jackson let Pham reach for the back-door handle, which was unlocked. Across the threshold, stairs went up to the left, and a walk-in freezer was on the right.

Pham trudged down the narrow hall and stepped into a kitchen. "I make some tea."

Jackson didn't argue. The old man had had a rough night. While Jackson waited in the dim space, Quince stuck his head in the back door. "Hey. What have we got?"

"I'm taking the business owner's statement now. The shooting victim is just outside. I've identified him as Buck Hinsic. Look for fire-starters, please." Jackson moved to let the old man slide by with a pot of tea, then turned back to Quince. "When the other team members get here, have them look for witnesses."

"Roger that."

He and Pham sat down in a back booth that reeked of greasy food and aging carpet. The old guy poured tea into tiny porcelain cups. Jackson gulped his, eager for the caffeine. "Tell me what happened. From the beginning." He pulled out his recorder, clicked it on, and set it in the middle of the table.

"I was reading and I hear noise outside. In back. So I get my new gun."

"What time?"

"I didn't check. Too scared. I just grabbed gun and go down." Pham took a delicate sip of tea with shaking hands. "Then I hear window break, so I run into restaurant and see flames." The old guy jumped up and moved toward a booth in the middle. Jackson grabbed the recorder and followed, noticing the broken window. He'd run right past it while focusing on finding the people involved. On the leather seat below it sat a broken bottle in the middle of a blackened area. A Molotov cocktail. Jackson could smell the gasoline.

"I use extinguisher to put out fire." Pham was animated now, talking loudly and gesturing as he re-enacted the scene. "Then I hear man in back near door. I run outside, worried of more flames. I see bad man with another bottle and yell for him to stop." His eyes went wide. "But he ran at me with arm raised. And I'm afraid to burn. So I shoot." Pham arched his shoulders forward as if to protect himself and looked distressed.

Jackson gestured for him to sit back down. When he had, Jackson asked, "How many times did you shoot?"

"Three. I miss first time, then use two hands." He was matter of fact now, but still shaking.

"The guy was running at you when you shot him?"

"Yes."

"You were afraid for your life?"

Pham touched his head. "Yes! He attack me before."

"Where's the bottle he was holding?"

"He drop and it roll away. I didn't look. Just call 911."

"Then what?"

161

"I wait for you." Pham locked eyes on him. "I do OK? Not go to jail?"

Jackson nodded.

Chapter 28

Thursday, July 11th, 6:00 a.m.

Evans woke to the alarm and swung her feet out of bed—touching something on the way. Startled, she glanced back. *Oh hell.* Todd had stayed the night. But he wasn't supposed to. That was the rule. They were just hanging out and having sex. She'd never intended to get serious about him. She reached over and shook his shoulder. "Hey, wake up." He'd shown up for a booty call late the night before, bribing her with dark chocolate and tequila. Now she had a headache. Or two.

He mumbled something she couldn't hear. Evans leaned in. "You have to get up. I'm leaving in twenty minutes."

"I have the day off. Let me sleep."

"Not here, please. Get moving." Evans decided to take a shower, giving him a few minutes. She didn't want to be a bitch, but this was important.

When she came out of the bathroom, he was sitting up but still groggy. And sexy. *Damn!* He was good-looking—and buff. She forced herself to look away and start getting dressed.

"Hey, babe. Come back to bed for a while." Even his voice was sexy.

Evans bit her lip. "I have to get to work." Quickly pulling on clothes, she kept her back turned to him.

"How's your case going?"

"Generally okay. But our suspect has disappeared and I

need to find him." Evans grabbed her weapon and a lightweight blazer, waiting until the last minute to put them on. "I'll make some coffee." She hurried into the kitchen and started a dark pot. Normally she worked out in the mornings with a kickboxing routine, but not today. While the coffee brewed, she put on makeup, then checked in with Todd. He was finally dressed.

He eased over and hugged her. "Hey, I'll be filming ads in the studio today. Take a break this afternoon and stop in for a while."

She decided to indulge him to make up for this morning. "Okay. Text me the location." Evans stepped back. "I really have to go."

Out on the road, she laughed quietly as she drove. She didn't really have a specific place to be, just a mission to find Griffen, who could be out of the country by now. But she would start by checking his house again—then knock on his sister's door, hoping to catch her before she left for work.

She took West Eleventh and drove by the burned-out building. The Golden Dragon had been one of the longest-operating restaurants in Eugene, and it was weird to see it gone. At least the arsonist hadn't gotten away with it. Lammers had called her to the second scene, but Jackson had sent her home early—because they didn't have to search for a perp and no charges would be pressed. Relieved that the hate-crime case was mostly over, she hoped to finally get some help with her homicide.

The first thing she noticed at the Bailey Hill location was that a newer white car—that looked like all the other new-car designs—was parked in front of the main home. But there was no vehicle at the tiny house. Evans parked, blocking the white car, then jogged up to the door and pounded. No sound came from inside. She grabbed her phone and messaged the woman too. If Lisa Priven had Instant Messenger, her cell might be pinging beside her bed.

Evans bounced on her feet as she waited. The caffeine was kicking in, and she hadn't burned off any energy with a workout. She pounded again. After a few minutes, she heard shuffling, then a woman called out, "Who is it?"

"Eugene Police. Open up!"

Finally, the door opened a crack. Priven, dressed only in a long sweatshirt, was forty-something and had purple streaks in her short brownish hair. "Is this about Jeff?"

"Yes. Where is he?"

"I don't know. He took off yesterday while I was at work, and I haven't seen him."

Evans didn't believe her, but she didn't have any leverage either. Griffen was smart enough to have turned off his phone. Even with the service-provider's help, they couldn't track him with cell towers. "This is important. Someone saw Jeff leave his ex-wife's house right before she was suffocated."

Priven gasped. "She was murdered? He told me she drank too much and took a sleeping pill. I thought she killed herself."

"The pathologist says someone held a pillow over her face." A detail she hadn't revealed to the press yet. But she would soon. They might need the public's help to find Griffen.

"I don't believe Jeff is capable of violence."

Everybody said that about their criminal relatives. "I want to search your house for him."

"Seriously? You can see that his jeep is gone. And the damn dog is gone too. You can tell by the quiet. Jeff is not here."

The sister had a point. If her brother would kill his wife over a dog, he wouldn't go on the run or hide out without the mutt. But she had to keep other suspects in mind. "Who else would want your sister-in-law dead?"

The woman's face crumpled. "I don't know. Jola and I weren't close. But still, this is so heartbreaking."

"Your brother needs to turn himself in. If he's innocent, he can try to prove it." Evans handed her a business card. "If Jeff contacts you, call me. Do not aid a wanted fugitive."

She started to walk away, then turned back. "I need to see the inside of his house. I assume you have a key."

Priven sighed. "Yes. But is it really necessary? He's not there."

"He's a murder suspect. I need all the information I can gather."

"Let me put on some pants." She shut the door.

Evans didn't move from the front step. She didn't intend to let this woman slide out and drive away while her back was turned. But the sister didn't try. She came out a few minutes later with a mug of tea in her hand and walked Evans over to the tiny house.

"It's probably a mess," Priven said, putting a key into the lock. "Jeff and Jola fought about that too." She opened the door and muttered, "Why did I share that?"

Evans hurried past her into the house. Clothes and empty sports-drink bottles cluttered the insanely small space. An empty pizza box sat on a mini coffee table. Evans ignored all of it and looked for a computer or phone or even a paper tablet that might have a list of tasks. Priven had followed her into the house and started straightening up.

"Don't! Please." Evans took photos of the mess. She wasn't sure if or why they would be used, but it seemed important to record the state of his home.

"That's a violation of his privacy," the sister complained.

"I only said you could look around. Make it fast, please."

"Okay." Evans needed her cooperation. She hoped the sister actually owned this house and had the authority to allow her access.

In the small space, her search went quickly but didn't provide anything useful. She turned to Priven, who was staying close by. "Can you tell if anything is missing? Such as luggage? Or favorite clothes?"

"No, but Jeff has a—" She stopped short.

"What? I need to find him." Time for a little emotional pressure. "Before another police officer does. My objective is to bring him in and question him. A patrol cop or sheriff's deputy might shoot him."

The sister's eyes flashed with worry. "I was just going to say that Jeff has some stuff stored at a friend's house. And by stuff, I mean bikes. Nothing helpful to you."

"Give me the friend's name and address."

"Jeff wouldn't stay there. The guy is married with young kids."

"Tell me anyway."

Evans keyed the information into her phone, thanked Priven for her cooperation, and headed for her car. On the way, a thought popped into her head, and she realized where she might find him.

Chapter 29

The alarm woke Jackson from a sound sleep. He slammed it off, hoping it hadn't woken Kera, then realized she was already out of bed. Groggy and dry-mouthed, he stumbled into the shower. He'd been up late dealing with Pham and waiting for the medical examiner to show up for Hinsic's body. Four hours of sleep hadn't been enough. But he had a meeting with Lammers in an hour.

Jackson hurried through his routine, aided by Kera, who made him coffee and toast. The boys were watching cartoons in the living room, and Jackson snuck out without engaging with them. He promised himself he would take a three-day weekend and spend it with the family. But at the moment, he was running late and feeling both exhausted and anti-social. A text from Lammers further darkened his mood: *Meet in chief's office.*

A half-hour later, he walked into Owens' corner office. Lammers sat in one of the visitor's chairs, and the chief was behind his desk. The man wasn't aging well and seemed to have shrunk another inch. But his expression was just as deadpan. "Jackson. Thanks for joining us."

"Of course, sir." *What did they want?*

"Give us an update on last night's call-out scenes."

"One Asian restaurant burned to the ground, and a man named Buck Hinsic was shot while trying to burn down another. The owner and shooter, Pham Thi Boc, was assaulted last week and says that Hinsic came at him last night and tried to kill him."

"Do you believe him?"

"Yes."

"And you think Hinsic set the fire at the other restaurant?" The chief was leading Jackson.

And he didn't care for it. "Yes. Most likely." The buildings were only a mile apart, and the M.O. was the same.

"What about the Jane Doe who was killed? Can we assume Hinsic assaulted her as well?"

Now he understood that was the point here. Jackson wasn't ready to make that claim, but he accepted that some of the evidence pointed in that direction. "Her name is Cam Le, and yes, that's a solid possibility."

"Then it's time to wrap up all the hate-crime cases. Go arrest a few more Homelanders to scare the group, then give a press conference naming Buck Hinsic as the vandal, arsonist, and murderer." The chief nodded. A done deal.

Jackson wasn't quite there. "I'd like to leave the homicide open until I at least finish examining all the evidence. Some things about the case don't add up."

"You're overthinking it."

That was his job! Jackson couldn't hold back. "Her body was likely dumped out of a vehicle. That suggests she knew the perp. And Cam Le swallowed a key to protect something. I just don't know what yet." The damn suitcase was still out there, but Quince was on his way to Portland now.

Lammers cut in. "I'm not sure how either of those things are relevant or rule out Buck Hinsic as the killer."

Jackson turned and gave her a disbelieving look.

But the chief had more to say. "Continuing the investigation on flimsy grounds is not a good use of our resources. Close it out. Then go help Evans with her homicide."

That sounded like an order. "Yes, sir." Annoyed, Jackson was ready to leave. "Is that it?"

"Keep up the good work."

Jackson nodded and rushed to the door. The chief hadn't set a timeline, so the press conference could wait at least until he'd seen the luggage and ruled it out.

Chapter 30

Evans called Schak on the drive over and asked him to meet her. He said "Will do" and ended the call without asking questions. She loved that about him. He trusted her and was treating her like the lead on this case. Fifteen minutes later, she parked in the victim's driveway. Griffen's vehicle wasn't visible, but he could have tucked it into the garage. Evans resisted the urge to pull her weapon and started around to the back of the house. If Griffen were a known criminal or had access to a gun, she would have waited for Schak. But this stop was just a hunch, and she started to think it was a waste of time. Now she wished she hadn't called Schak.

As she hustled across the backyard, a dog barked inside the house. One high-pitched but muffled yap, then quiet again. Griffen was here.

Evans stopped at the sliding door opening into the bedroom, where she had entered the house the first time. The curtains were closed, blocking her visibility. She grabbed the door handle, called out "Police," and lunged inside.

Griffen lay on his ex-wife's bed, with the little dog on his belly. The animal tried to stand, gave another muffled yap, then collapsed back down.

Evans stared at the suspect, who was struggling to open his eyes.

Were they both drugged?

"Griffen!" Evans scanned the scene, looking for pill

bottles or weapons. She didn't see any.

The man opened his eyes and tried to sit up. "Leave me alone."

"Are you drugged?"

"Maybe."

Schak bolted through the open door, his gun drawn. He took in the scenario and quickly holstered his weapon. "What's going on?"

"I think he's trying to kill himself. Call 911."

"No." Griffen tried to sit up again. "I want to die."

"We can't let that happen," Evans said. "Even if you killed your ex-wife." But she wasn't sure why not. He faced a lifetime sentence in prison.

"I didn't do it. I loved Jola." Griffen eased himself back down. The dog didn't move.

"What did you take?" The paramedics would want to know.

"You have to believe me." The man's words were slow and slurred now. "But I can't face prison. I can't put my sister through a trial."

Evans had a flash of doubt. Was he innocent? A man in the wrong place at the wrong time? So unlikely.

Schak ended his 911 call. "Let's get him up and walk him around." He stepped toward Griffen.

"Good plan." Evans grabbed the suspect's legs and pulled them sideways and off the bed.

Schak squatted low and lifted Griffen's torso, putting his own shoulder into it. Evans grabbed the man's other arm and pulled. When they had him upright, they each sat on a side and put an arm around him.

"Ready?" Schak asked.

"Yep."

They heaved him to his feet, his body sagging and lifeless. Evans was glad he was a skinny cyclist. "Move your legs," she commanded.

They walked Griffen around the room, mostly dragging him. After a minute, he seemed to revive a little. "I swear I didn't kill her," he cried out. "But I can't prove it."

"Then why kill yourself? Innocent people don't do that."

Griffen managed a bitter laugh. "But they die in prison all the time."

Evans had another flash of doubt.

"Why come here?" Schak asked. "That looks like guilt too." They kept Griffen moving around the room.

"No guilt. Just love. I wanted to be close to Jola."

"Who else would want her dead?" Evans asked. She couldn't let go of one suspect without having another.

"Ask her sister." Griffen's legs suddenly buckled.

Evans heard a siren in the distance and breathed a sigh of relief.

Chapter 31

Sophie walked out of the employee meeting feeling angry and bitter, as usual. More cost-cutting, more pressure. It had been going on for years. The newspaper's quality had been slipping in tandem, and they hadn't won any awards recently or picked up new readers. She wasn't even sure she was grateful to still have a job. The anxiety of knowing any moment at work could be her last was eclipsing her joy in covering the news.

She hurried back to her desk, not even wanting to commiserate with other employees. Feeling strangely liberated, she called the state prison where Jason McCarthy was being held. She might as well work on her own stories. The man who answered sounded bored. Sophie asked to speak to his supervisor. "I'm a reporter with the Willamette News," she added, hoping he had some respect for, or fear of, the media.

Without comment, he put her through to another office. While she waited, Sophie checked the prison's visiting hours. A session was scheduled for late that afternoon.

A woman answered this time. "Anna Nelson, Assistant Superintendent. How can I help you?"

"I'm a reporter, and I'd like to interview Jason McCarthy. I filled out an application a few days ago."

"Repeat your name, please."

Sophie did so and waited.

"You've been approved, but his acceptance paperwork hasn't been processed yet. That may take a few days."

Which meant next week. "Can you expedite that last part and let me see him today? I'm on deadline for a piece I'm writing about his father." She paused for emphasis. "Dennis McCarthy, presidential candidate."

"Well, that's news." The woman sucked in air through her teeth. "You're not coming here to write a hit piece about our facility?"

"Oh no. This is a political family story."

"I'll track down his signed form and get it into the system."

"Soon? I'd like to make his visiting session at five."

The woman laughed. "I'll do my best." Then she clicked off.

Sophie checked the time. She'd have to leave soon to make the drive to Madras on time. What if she got out there and they didn't let her in? Four-plus hours round trip for nothing. She would call the prison again from the road and check for an update. Feeling more upbeat, she checked her to-do list. *Get details on new case.*

Hoping Jasmine would know something, she pressed a speed-dial icon to reach her. Jasmine picked up, sounding weary. "Hey, Sophie. I'm a little overwhelmed. Can I call you back?"

"Give me something on Jola Shaffer, please. Cause of death would be a good start."

"Intentionally suffocated," Jasmine whispered. "Husband is suspect and on the run. I have to go."

Now that was a news story. Sophie grinned, opened a file, and wrote a lead. She already knew the husband's name and that the couple was divorcing because she'd checked out Shaffer's page on Facebook. She just needed another detail or two. She stopped writing and sent an online message to the woman's sister to see if she would respond.

She also called Evans, hoping to flesh out the story, but the detective didn't answer. Disappointed, Sophie left her a message: "Please call me about Jola Shaffer, the new murder victim. I'd like to confirm a few details."

Sophie was optimistic Evans would get back to her. They'd bonded, sort of, over a case a few years earlier, and Evans had become friendlier and more forthcoming over time. But she was probably busy tracking down leads. Sophie would try again this evening. Maybe offer to meet for a drink. They'd done that once or twice.

After fleshing out her story—with mostly filler—Sophie saved the file. She loaded Facebook again and searched Jola Shaffer's posts for links to her ex-husband. An easy task. Jeff Griffen, she soon learned, worked at Hutch's as a bike mechanic. Since the boyfriend, husband, or ex was usually the guilty perp, Evans decided to include him in the story.

Her phone rang, and she glanced at the number. It was vaguely familiar, so she answered the call. "Sophie Speranza."

"This is Rick Brantley again. We talked earlier about Dennis McCarthy's service in Viet Nam."

He sounded even drunker now. "Thanks again."

"I never told you the main reason I hate McCarthy."

"I'm listening."

"There's no nice way to put this." A long pause. "Like a lot of guys, McCarthy raped Viet women. It disgusted me."

A sick feeling flooded Sophie's stomach. "You witnessed it?"

"He bragged about it."

She needed confirmation from another source. "Who else was in your unit that could verify this?"

"They're all dead now."

"All of them? I just need one person to confirm."

"Then confront McCarthy." The old vet hung up.

Chapter 32

After watching the ambulance drive off, Evans turned to Schak. "I hate to break this to you, but you get to deal with the dog." She tried not to laugh at his distressed look.

"Oh, come on. Let's at least flip for it."

Scooter had thrown up while they waited for the paramedics, then perked up a bit, so she thought the dog would be all right. "Lammers said I could run this case, so I'm delegating the task to you." Evans grinned. "Hey, I bagged the vomit for evidence, so I did my part." She had spotted a couple of partially digested capsules in the mess and decided to preserve them. The glamorous life of a detective.

"What do I do with the critter?" Schak's forehead glistened with sweat. Dragging Griffen around to keep him awake had been work for both of them.

"Take the dog out to his sister's house. Or to a vet. Your call." They'd never had anyone try to commit suicide along with their pet. Some people took out their kids when they decided to end their lives, but this was a first. "I have to find Shaffer's sister again and see if she knows what the hell Griffen was talking about."

"Keep me posted. I'm going back in for the mutt." Schak gave her a dirty look.

Evans smiled sweetly, waved, and hurried to her car. Once inside, she let out the laugh she'd been suppressing. But it faded quickly. Frustration and guilt overwhelmed her.

What if Griffen hadn't killed his ex-wife? What if she had almost driven an innocent man to suicide? Feeling apprehensive, she called Carene Zindler, the victim's sister. No answer, so she left a message: "I need to ask you something important. Please call ASAP." Evans sent a similar text, then checked the time. It was after two. No wonder she was starving.

But before taking a break, she called Jackson out of habit. "Hey, it's Evans. Do you want an update on the Shaffer case?"

"A brief one, sure."

"We found Griffen, the victim's ex-husband and likely suspect, and stopped him from killing himself. But he still claims to be innocent."

"That's a little odd." Jackson sounded distracted.

Evans laughed. "You think that's weird, wait until you hear the details."

"At our next meeting."

She decided to share her doubts. "I'm starting to think Griffen might not be guilty, but I don't have any other motives or ideas."

"Where is he?"

"The hospital, under guard."

"Then let's start over and look at everything again. I'll help. My case is closed."

Evans loved him for all of that. "Thanks. That's what I wanted to hear. If we still come up with Griffen, then great, case solved."

"We'll all meet up later. See you then."

Later, while in the drive-up line to buy a burrito, Evans remembered her promise to Todd. Not exactly a promise, but she would humor him anyway. She was due for a break—

before the team started fresh to find a motive for Jola Shaffer's murder.

Evans ate half her meal on the drive downtown, then set it aside. The studio was on Sixth Avenue, not far from the old department. But she couldn't visualize the building. When she arrived, she realized it had been renovated recently. And apparently, it now held a studio for filming TV ads and videos. But the words *film* and *TV* didn't mean anything anymore. Everything was digital. Evans texted Todd, telling him she'd arrived, then popped in a breath mint and headed inside.

The receptionist greeted her warmly and led her down a hallway to a room in the back of the building. The front section was partitioned by a heavy accordion-style moveable wall and held only a few chairs, a coat rack, and a set of lockers. She waited in a chair until Todd pushed back the curtain near the wall and gestured for her to come in. He gave her a quick kiss, then led her into a dark, cavernous room, lit only by monitors and blinking camera lights. Now that she'd seen it, she was ready to leave. The room made her uneasy.

"'Just stay back here and watch. We're getting ready to capture another segment." Todd sounded excited.

She was happy for him but wishing she could exit gracefully. "I have to go soon. We have a new development in the case."

"What do you mean?" His pretty face was hard to read in the semi-darkness.

"It's too complicated for the moment. Go. Make your commercial."

Todd hesitated, then shrugged and headed into the maze of cameras, thick floor cables, and overhead light stands. He took a spot in front of a big screen and said, "Ready."

Lights flooded him, and a woman called, "Action."

Todd's sexy voice filled the room. He introduced himself and his occupation, taking pride in his community service. Then he introduced his father, "Dennis McCarthy, the most qualified candidate for president in decades."

Evans suppressed a smirk. He was laying it on a bit thick, but that's what political ads did.

She tuned out for a moment and checked her phone. No response from Jola's sister. An alarming thought hit her. What if Griffen had meant that her sister wanted Jola dead? Evans was glad she hadn't mentioned the actual issue when she'd contacted Zindler.

Todd's speech abruptly caught her attention. *What was he saying?* Evans leaned forward and tuned back in.

"We can't allow this country to become a safe haven for illegals." His tone was harsher now, not as sexy. "As president, my father will not allow sanctuary cities. He'll cut off funding to those that don't comply."

What the hell? And what kind of funding? Apparently, Todd wasn't worried about his own job; as a deputy, he worked for the county, not Eugene.

"Dennis McCarthy will also send troops to the border when needed. We believe the current president's decision to withhold military support for this crisis is unpatriotic." Todd paused, as if waiting for an applause line.

Oh brother. Evans realized they hadn't talked politics that much. Shoptalk about crimes and cases usually dominated their brief conversations. But she didn't agree with him on this issue. Military personnel shouldn't be politicized.

But Todd was on a roll. "Our current gun laws have to be scaled back," Todd boomed. "And my father has the courage and political capital to get that done. He's a military veteran who fought for our rights, and he won't let special interest groups and snowflake liberals dominate our decisions, suppress individual rights, and sidetrack our future."

Time to go. Evans stood and hurried out. Most of the officers she knew, herself included, wanted stricter gun control. More guns meant more dead cops. She found it hard to believe Todd couldn't see that.

In her car, she struggled to push her thoughts and emotions aside. She would deal with the Todd situation later. Right now, she had to focus on this case. She checked her phone. Zindler had texted: *I'll call you later.*

Not soon enough. Evans texted back: *I need to know now. Where are you?*

Evans reached for the starter, ready to move but unsure of what came next. The hospital? Maybe they'd revived Griffen enough to answer her questions coherently this time. On the street, she headed for the freeway, assuming Griffen had been taken to North McKenzie in Springfield. Stopped in construction traffic, she glanced at her phone. Zindler had texted: *I'm at Embers.*

Another bar. *The woman liked to drink socially.* Evans pulled out of the lane she was in and kept driving west. The dive bar was on the edge of town, not far from the railroad tracks. According to old-timers, it had been serving alcohol and steak to middle-aged drunks for as long as they could remember.

Evans gunned her engine, feeling wired and anxious. Too much coffee with no exercise, a case that suddenly made no sense, and a boyfriend who was politically too extreme. Maybe she should deal with that issue sooner rather than later. It might give her some peace of mind. She would miss the sex, but only until she started dating someone else. The men were all just friends with benefits. Jackson had broken her heart, and she didn't think she'd ever fall in love again.

The Embers appeared on her right, a boxy tan building with a sloped parking lot—which had to be challenging for the drunks after 'last call.' Evans parked and called Todd, knowing he was busy and wouldn't answer. She left a message, trying to sound soft and casual: "Hey, Todd. Today was interesting. But it made me realize our politics are too far apart to keep seeing each other. I'm sorry. I wanted to do this in person, but with my schedule, that could have taken days." She didn't know how to end it, so she simply said "Take care" and ended the message.

After a deep breath, she climbed out and looked around for the cigarette smoke she smelled. Someone who had just passed by?

Evans texted Zindler and went inside. But the woman either didn't get her message or didn't care. So Evans had to search for the sister in the darkened space and finally found her in a closet-like room playing video poker. Hearing her approach, the woman spun on a tall stool. "You again."

"Yep. I want justice for your sister. And Jeff Griffen swears he didn't kill her."

"He's a pig." Zindler's blurry eyes and sagging facial skin indicated she'd been here a while. Did she always drink like this or was she numbing her grief?

"I asked Jeff who else would want Jola dead. He said to ask you."

Zindler pulled back with eyes wide. "I don't know what he's talking about."

Evans wanted to believe her. But maybe she didn't realize what she knew. "Did Jola have important information about someone? Had she ever witnessed a crime? Stolen someone's boyfriend?" Evans was grasping for any motive she could think of.

"Hell yeah, she witnessed a crime. She was raped."

The counselor had mentioned Jola's anxiety about it. "I thought her attacker went to jail. Did he threaten her for sending him away?" Inmates did manage to pay criminals on the outside to take care of business for them.

Zindler blinked a few times. "Oh fuck. I can tell you, but I just don't believe it's related." She gulped the rest of her drink and slid off the stool, wagging a finger. "I think Jeff Griffen was so freaked about the dog, he decided to end the fight once and for all. My poor baby sister." She sobbed, then hiccupped and tried to focus her eyes.

Evans tried again. "Just tell me about the other thing and let me decide if it's related."

Zindler's shoulders sagged. "It was eight years ago."

"Tell me anyway."

"Jola kinda thinks the man who confessed to her rape didn't actually do it."

What?

The tipsy woman tried to get back on her stool and failed. Her speech was getting sloppy too. "But Jola was pretty drunk when it happened and scared to testify. So she went along to keep her name out of the news."

"That doesn't make sense. Why would someone confess to a rape they didn't commit?"

"Hell if I know." Zindler abruptly grabbed her mouth, spun around, and vomited in the corner.

Oh hell. Twice in one day. Evans wanted to run from the room. Instead, she asked, "Can I give you a ride home?"

Zindler popped back up. "No. I'm fine. And I'm done talking to you."

"What's the name of the rapist who went to prison?"

But Zindler was walking away and waved off the question.

Evans' phone rang in her pocket, and she snatched it up, recognizing the number for the hospital.

Chapter 33

An officer sat outside the entrance. Evans nodded at him, pushed aside the sliding door, and walked into the hospital room. Griffen was awake but groggy. He groaned when he saw her. "Leave me alone."

Evans walked over to the bed. "I'm just checking to make sure you're okay." *Sort of true.*

"Well, I'm not. I feel like shit, and I'm suspected of homicide. Me." Trying not to cry, he pointed to his own chest. "I don't even kill bugs."

"But you were at your estranged wife's home right before she was murdered. You see how this looks to me." Evans kept her voice soft.

"Yes. And I don't stand a chance against a biased prosecutor and a sympathetic jury." Tears rolled down his cheeks. "Why couldn't you just let me die? I can't face the shame of a murder trial. And I'll never survive in prison."

He was either a terrific actor or a very unlucky man. But she'd been fooled by criminal manipulators before. "What time did you leave Jola's house?"

"I told you. Around nine-thirty."

"Did you buy gas or stop at a store on the way home?" She was thinking about security cameras providing an alibi for him.

"No."

"Did you make a phone call or send any texts that

evening?" She made a mental note to subpoena his phone records.

"No." He wiped his face and tried to look composed. "But I talked to my sister. She stopped by my little house to check on me."

Not a solid alibi. "Why would she do that?"

"She knew I was struggling. Jola and I were both prone to depression. That was part of the initial attraction."

Evans didn't understand, but it wasn't important. There was more she needed to know. "Why did you go back into Jola's house?"

Griffen squeezed his eyes shut and was quiet for a long moment. "I wanted to find Scooter's medication."

He was holding something back, and this probably wasn't about the dog. "What kind?"

"Pain pills."

Evans got a glimmer of the truth. "You mean opioids."

"Yes. Scooter had surgery a while back, and the vet prescribed them for his recovery. But Jola wouldn't give them to the dog or let me."

"So you found the stash and took them all at once, hoping to commit suicide?"

He nodded. "I wanted Jola's Ambien, but it was all gone. And there wasn't enough of the dog's meds." More tears rolled down his face. "So I borrowed some fentanyl tabs from a friend who has cancer."

"And gave some to the dog too." She knew she sounded disgusted and didn't care.

"Just his own pills." He sat up, his eyes wide with worry. "Is Scooter okay?"

"Yes. He's with your sister."

"I can't believe I did that to him." Griffen began to sob.

After a minute, Evans walked out, unable to take any more.

Chapter 34

At his desk, Jackson downed a can of Diet Dr. Pepper, enjoying the cold sweetness. His brain and body were both overheated. Sunlight had poured through the tall windows all day, making his workspace too warm, and the chief had fried his nerves with his order to close the murder case. But Jackson had no real choice in the matter. Time to shift gears.

He found Evans' case notes on their shared server and read through what she'd learned about the victim, Jola Shaffer. The details were scant. He checked the timestamp on the file and realized she'd posted it the night before. Evans had been out in the field all day and had only checked in with him once, so he hoped she had an update. Feeling out of the loop and ready to be useful, Jackson sent a group text to his task force: *Meet in conference room in one hour. Text if problem.*

Quince was his other concern. He'd been gone all day too and, so far, was unreachable. Jackson hoped the issue was simply a delay in chasing down the victim's luggage, maybe followed by a dead cell battery. He leaned back in his chair and closed his eyes, letting the facts of the Shaffer case roll around in his head without intentionally trying to steer or mesh them. Sometimes he got lucky, and his subconscious made connections and realizations for him. But without much detail, he wasn't optimistic. Either way, he needed the mental break.

Ten minutes later, he caught himself just as he was about to doze off. Jackson snapped his feet to the floor and stood to stretch. His only new thought was that Cam Le and Jola Shaffer were around the same age. Which meant nothing. He hadn't been trying to connect the cases. He'd been trying to find a new and distinct motive for each of their deaths. If Cam Le hadn't been killed by a white nationalist, then who and why? If Jola Shaffer hadn't been killed by her ex-husband, then who?

The team needed a good brainstorming session. More physical evidence would be helpful too. Jackson checked the time, then made two calls, ordering sandwiches and coffee from a nearby bistro. He took a walk outside while he waited for the meeting to start and called Kera.

"Hey, Jackson. You must be having a busy day."

"Two cases that have both gone sideways. So we're having a task force meeting to brainstorm and start fresh."

"You'll have dinner at the meeting?"

"Yeah, so don't wait for me."

"I think I'll take the kids out to eat. We haven't done that in a while."

"I'm sorry to miss it." He visualized his family having fun without him, and his heart hurt. "Any update on finding a rental?"

"I'm just waiting for you to have time to look at the one I like best."

"Does it have a spot where I can set up a small home office?"

"It does. That's at the top of my checklist."

"Then just fill out the paperwork and I'll sign it. I trust you."

A long pause.

"I love you, Wade."

His heart burst with joy. "I love you, Kera."

"Now you have to get going, right?" She laughed.

"I do. I'll see you tonight."

"I'll be waiting." She ended the call.

She'd used her sexy voice. *Damn.* He hoped he wasn't too exhausted.

He hustled into the department, ready for the air conditioning again. At his desk, he printed a copy of each murder-case file and crossed the wide hall to the conference room.

No one had arrived yet, so he updated the neglected whiteboards and paid for the food when it arrived. Evans and Schak came in together as the delivery guy was leaving. They all sat down at the same time.

"Is Quince coming?" Evans asked.

"I hope so. He drove to Portland to retrieve Cam Le's luggage—which could turn out to be a total waste of time. But I thought he'd be back by now."

"Try texting him."

"I have, but I will again." Jackson sent a quick message, then looked at Evans. "What have you got? Does it need to go on the whiteboard?"

Evans stood and moved to the front. "Our main suspect, Jeff Griffen, is in the hospital recovering from an overdose. He went to his wife's house to retrieve some of the dog's pain medication and borrowed a few fentanyl pills from a friend who has cancer—then took them all at once. Except what he gave the dog." She rolled her eyes. "And yes, a police officer is guarding him." She jotted brief notes on the board, then turned back with a funny smile. "The dog survived too."

"Yeah, Scooter's fine," Schak said dryly.

None of that really mattered. "Did Griffen confess to killing his wife?" Jackson asked.

"No. He says he wanted to die rather than face a trial and life in prison." Evans shrugged. "I can see myself making that choice. I mean about prison."

Jackson had mixed feelings. And more questions. "Doesn't that seem like bullshit though? Suicide is more likely related to guilt and trying to control the situation."

Schak snorted. "I'm with you on that. The fact that he would kill his beloved dog rather than let someone else have it is a sign of a control freak. I think Griffen felt that way about his ex-wife too. He's guilty and we just need to prove it."

"Have you impounded his vehicle? Seized his phone?" Jackson asked. "We need mileage, locations, and everything we can to nail him.

Evans nodded. "I'm on all of it." She hesitated for a moment. "But we need to look at another possibility too."

"What?" Jackson and Schak spoke at the same time.

"Shaffer was raped eight years ago. And for some reason, she doesn't believe the guy who pleaded to the crime is actually the perp."

That made no sense. "How do you know this?"

"Her sister told me. And Shaffer's counselor confirmed the rape and Jola's PTSD connected to it."

Schak leaned back and crossed his arms. "Did she give you names? Dates? Details we can check out?"

Evans sighed. "Not yet. The sister, Carene Zindler, was drunk and vomiting. Then the hospital called, so I went out to interrogate Griffen again."

Jackson made a decision. "If you can question the sister when she's sober and get real information, we'll pursue the lead. But I think it's a waste of time." He put that lead on the back burner. "Tracking down the evidence we need to convict Griffen has to be our priority. If we can place his vehicle and his phone at the scene at the time of death, that's all we need."

Evans nodded again. "We have a witness who saw a similar vehicle at the house at eleven-thirty. And the neighbor says a man was driving. But he won't make a definitive ID."

"We can still put him on the stand," Schak added.

Jackson's phone rang on the table. *Jasmine Parker.* Thank goodness. They needed some tangible evidence. He answered and put her on speaker. "Jackson here with the team. What have you got for us?"

"Sorry, not much. The Cam Le case is a dead end. We collected a few cigarette butts from under the dumpster and sent the DNA to the lab, but it hasn't come back."

Evans jumped in. "What about the Shaffer house? Did you find anything useful?"

"I wasn't quite done," Parker snapped. "But in short, the answer is no. No prints in the bedroom except the husband and wife. We checked her three prescription bottles too. The contents match the labels, except the Ambien bottle, which was empty. So we don't think anyone switched out her medicine. The preliminary lab analysis indicates she had alcohol and a central-nervous-system suppressant in her system, and everything indicates they were voluntarily ingested."

Jackson hadn't seen the autopsy report, but he'd heard the conclusion. "What made the pathologist call it suffocation?"

"She had pillow fibers in her lungs. But not many. She was already quite sedated and died quickly."

An unsettling thought popped into Jackson's head.

"Would she have died anyway? If someone hadn't held a pillow over her face?"

"Maybe. We have no way of assessing that."

Schak let out another snort. "So if Griffen had left her alone, he might have come out all right."

They were all quiet for a moment. Then Evans said, "Griffen told me they both suffered from depression and that was part of their original attraction."

"Can I finish my report?" Parker sounded annoyed again.

"Of course."

"Here's the interesting thing. I'm not saying it's useful or means much, but I found it worth noting." She took a sip of something before continuing. "We found a particular pollen on the victim—"

"Her name is Cam Le," Jackson interjected. The poor woman deserved that.

"Got it. Anyway, the pollen on her clothes is from a filbert tree, which we found near the crime scene. What might be interesting is that we found a trace of the same tree pollen on the pillow used to smother Jola Shaffer."

Questions flooded Jackson's brain. "Is there a filbert tree in Shaffer's yard? Or neighborhood?"

"No. But the pollen is common to the whole area and could have been on the pillow for weeks."

The warm months in Eugene were so pollen-filled it was hard to see how this was relevant. "Thanks, Parker. It's an interesting observation. If these cases had any overlap at all, the trace evidence could be significant. But they don't."

"That's what I thought. I'll get back to you with DNA results when we have them." She clicked off.

Jackson checked the time again. *Where the hell was Quince?*

Chapter 35

Listening to music made the drive to Madras go quickly. The bright blue sky and gorgeous green wilderness kept her smiling, and the snow-capped mountain peaks were photo-worthy. Sophie stopped halfway in the town of Sisters to pee and call the prison. After being assured she was on the visitors' list, she got back into her Scion and headed east at the junction.

An hour later, she arrived at the isolated prison right on schedule and parked in the huge, half-filled lot. The surrounding area was brown, empty, and desolate. She tried not to let the landscape bring her down. Leaving everything but her ID and some quarters in the car, as instructed, she walked up to the main doors. They opened and closed automatically, trapping her inside a small waiting area until the next set of doors opened. Inside the facility, a group of visitors stood in line, waiting to be checked in. She joined the line and observed the process, hoping to get everything right and breeze through.

But a young woman kept getting stopped by the metal detector. The desk deputy suggested the visitor take off her underwire bra. Mumbling under her breath, the woman headed for the bathroom, and the line moved forward. Sophie put her hoop earrings, her bag of quarters, and her ID into a plastic basket and walked through the security arch. No buzzing sound. She smiled at the second deputy, who grinned back and opened the interior door.

The visiting room held twenty or so round tables, with four chairs at each. An inmate sat at each table with his guests. For some, only an older man or woman had come to visit, but for others, the chairs were full. Sometimes with young kids. The back wall was lined with vending machines, and now she knew what the quarters were for.

Sophie stopped at the greeter's station and announced who she was here to see. The helper inmate escorted her across the crowded room. As she walked between tables, she noticed all of the inmates wore jeans and faded-denim shirts. Also, three of the chairs at each table were green, and the fourth was red—and the inmate always sat in the red chair. *Interesting.* In case someone tried to pull a switch? The visitor guidelines had warned against wearing denim of any kind.

"Jason is on the end." Her guide pointed and turned back.

Sophie sat down across from a good-looking man with a charming smile. Not even his chipped tooth and prison haircut diminished his appeal. She reached over and shook his hand. "Sophie Speranza, reporter. Thanks for seeing me."

"I'm Jason. Thanks for coming. I haven't had a visitor since my mom died."

Gaining her sympathy already. Like most criminals, he was likely a manipulator. "I'm sorry for your loss." She wished like hell she'd been able to bring in a recorder. Or even a tablet and pen. "When do you get released?"

"Two years, three months, and twelve days." Jason McCarthy smiled softly, but his eyes were wary.

"I assume you know your father is running for president?"

"Yes. He writes to me and puts money on my books. But doesn't visit."

"How do you feel about his candidacy?"

The inmate shrugged, then grinned. "As president, he could pardon me." Then Jason laughed. "But he won't."

"Does your dad ever talk about his service in Viet Nam?"

Jason leaned back and narrowed his eyes. "I made a mental list of the things I thought you'd ask me, but that wasn't on it."

"The subject came up from a protestor at a political rally. The guy gave me his uncle's name and number, so I called him." Sophie paused, but Jason didn't react. "His army buddy didn't have nice things to say about your dad."

The inmate nodded. "People either love him or hate him."

"And you?" she asked.

"Both." Another charming smile. "I'll bet you hate his politics."

"Pretty much." She smiled back. "But this piece isn't meant as a hit job. It's a personality profile. I want to know the man behind the campaign speeches."

"No, you don't. He's all about money and power and notoriety now. His new wife brought that out in him."

Sophie had intended to bring up the subject of McCarthy, as an army private, killing his commander, but she changed her mind. His son wouldn't be able to confirm or deny it, and the fact, or rumor, would just cause him pain. "What else should I know about Dennis McCarthy, the candidate? What does he read? What are his hobbies? Was he a fun dad?"

Jason laughed. "I like you."

"I'm glad." Sophie gave him a look. "Will you answer the question?"

"Sure. He reads nonfiction, mostly biographies of famous men. He golfs, of course. And watches old movies." Jason cracked his knuckles as he talked. "As a father, he could be fun. He took us to Ems baseball games when we were young, and I loved that. But he could be a dick too."

"Like what?"

"Quick temper and no flexibility. Everything had to be his way."

Sophie made notes in her head, hoping the details would stick. "Oh hey, do you want something to eat or drink?" She picked up the plastic bag of quarters and smiled.

"Sure. I'd like a Pepsi. But you have to go get it. I'm not allowed to leave the table once I sit down."

Sophie scooted over to the nearest vending machine and bought two sodas, indulging herself in Diet 7-Up. Back at the table, Jason leaned toward her. "Can I tell my story?"

"Of course." She unscrewed the lid on her bottle.

"Yes, I assaulted a man. He screwed my girlfriend, so I beat him senseless." Jason's mouth twisted into a smirk. "Actually, he was already senseless. I just beat him down." He stopped and scowled. "Don't look at me like that. The man knew better. And at least I didn't hit Dana."

"I didn't mean to judge." She softened her expression. "Dana was your girlfriend?"

"I caught them fucking. He's lucky I didn't kill him."

Surprised by all of it, Sophie regrouped. Jason McCarthy had pleaded to a prosecution deal, so she'd found only a few simple facts when she'd googled his name. And she had assumed the rape and assault were associated. But now she didn't know. "What about your girlfriend? How did she fare?"

"I told you. I never touched her. Never spoke to her again."

Sophie didn't know how to ask diplomatically, so she just blurted it out. "But you pleaded guilty to rape. Who was the victim?"

"A friend of the family." Hands on the table, he leaned

toward her. "But I didn't rape her. My father paid me to confess since I was going to prison anyway." A bitter laugh. "He pressured me to."

How strange. Sophie didn't understand. "What about the victim? Didn't she contradict you?" Victims often wouldn't even give their names, so maybe the woman hadn't dared go public.

"She was drunk at the time. And apparently couldn't tell one good-looking guy from another."

Sophie was starting to think the whole story was bullshit. He was just a prisoner having second thoughts about his confession and using her to get some attention or relief. "I'm not sure about any of this." But she was curious. "So if not you, who is the rapist? Do you know?"

"I sure do."

Chapter 36

Jackson glanced at his case notes. All that was left to discuss were his concerns about Cam Le's death. A case he'd been ordered to close out. But he knew his team would want to know everything. And it wouldn't be the first time they'd worked a case on their own time—against orders. So he launched in with an update. "After Buck Hinsic's crime spree and death last night, the chief told me to close out all the hate crimes. The assaults, the homicide, and the fires. I argued to keep the murder case open but to no avail."

"Let me guess. You have to give a press conference too, right?" Evans rolled her eyes.

"Yes. But I'm stalling. Two elements of this case still bother me." Jackson stood and moved toward the whiteboard. He didn't know if he would add to it again, but he felt restless. "The key in the victim's stomach, for example. What does it open and why did she swallow it? I don't feel right about shutting down the investigation until I understand that."

"What if you never do?" Schak shrugged. "Some deaths are like that. Remember the Danebo murder? Hundreds of hours going over every inch of the man's house and life. No motive or suspect ever surfaced. At least we have a viable person to pin this homicide on."

"I know. But there's still a piece—"

Quince burst into the room, looking rattled and windblown. He even had a stain on his shirt, which was totally unlike him. He heaved the missing suitcase—a small gray wheeled carryon—onto the table and plopped into a chair. "This has been one hell of a day."

"Why didn't you answer my texts?" Jackson asked.

"My phone died early this morning. And the air conditioning in my car quit so I had to open a window." He gestured at his messy hair. "And I sat in traffic for two frigging hours just to get out of the Portland area. Before that, I drove all over hell trying to find the construction site, which was not where I'd been told." Quince noticed the food and coffee in the middle of the table and reached for both. He tore into a sandwich and talked with his mouth full. "But there's a locked folder in a zippered pocket inside this luggage. Do we still have the key?"

A rush of adrenaline charged up Jackson's spine. He dug in his satchel for the evidence bag containing the key, then pushed out of his chair.

"Don't get your hopes up," Schak cautioned. "She probably just had family photos or letters from a dead loved one."

Jackson unzipped the suitcase, flopped the lid back, then unzipped the wide compartment in the underside of the lid. He slipped his hand in and retrieved a tan-colored folder made of thin cardboard. The tiny key fit into the flat embedded lock—which served no real purpose. He could have cut into the folder with a steak knife.

Inside was a collection of papers. Jackson flipped through, handing them to team members as he went along. On the bottom of the stack was what looked like a birth certificate. Much of the text was foreign, likely Vietnamese, but two English words stood out.

What did they mean?

Chapter 37

Evans' phone chirped in her pocket, a non-department contact. She glanced at the ID and shook her head. "Sophie Speranza." She rejected the call, set the device on the table, and stared at the document Jackson had just handed her. It had a fancy border and groups of text boxes that held information written in another language. Now her phone beeped, indicating a text. She glanced at the screen. Sophie again. Evans opened and read the message: *Please call me. This is important. And delicate. And possibly time-sensitive.*

Evans caught Jackson's attention. "Sophie is really trying to connect with me. She says it's critical."

"You'd better take it. Sometimes she's melodramatic to get what she wants, but sometimes she comes through for us."

Evans pressed redial and put the phone on speaker. "Sophie, we're at a task force meeting so make this quick. What have you got?"

"It's complicated." The connection was scratchy, and they could hear road noise in the background. "I'm driving back from a prison in Madras, where I visited an inmate named Jason McCarthy. And I've been calling you for an hour!" Sophie was clearly worked up.

Evans' gut tightened. *McCarthy was a common name,* she told herself. "What's this about?"

"I'm covering Dennis McCarthy's campaign for president, and Jason is his son."

Oh shit. This was about Todd's family. She hadn't known he had a brother in prison. Apparently they hadn't done enough talking. Another wave of panic. Had Todd listened to her break-up message? Evans tried to calm her escalating pulse. "How is this relevant to us?"

"I'm getting there." Sophie sounded like she was trying to settle down too. "It kind of relates to a recent homicide, but you need the backstory first."

Dread filled Evans' stomach. She glanced at her team members, who were leaning forward with wide eyes. They didn't know she was—or had been—dating Deputy Todd McCarthy.

Sophie continued. "Jason told me he didn't commit the rape he pleaded guilty to. He says his father coerced him—and paid him—to take the rap for it."

Oh no. Evans felt sick. She'd just heard a story like this—and it was starting to make sense. She didn't want to hear the rest of Sophie's information, but she had to. "Why would Dennis McCarthy, our current governor, do something like that?"

"Because he wanted to protect his other son. Jason was already going to prison for assault, so his dad pushed the rape onto his record too."

There it was. Todd's brother had accused him of rape. Evans didn't want to believe it. "When did this supposedly happen and who is the victim?" But she already knew. A drunk woman in a bar had told her earlier that day. Considering the way Jackson and Schak were looking at her, they understood too.

"Jola Shaffer, the woman who was murdered recently," Sophie said. "Dennis claims his brother, Todd McCarthy, is the one who raped her. All three were acquaintances, and the assault happened at a party. But Jola was really intoxicated and didn't go to the police until later. She talked to an acquaintance in the department and described her attacker, claiming it was either Todd or Dennis McCarthy. Apparently, they look a lot alike."

A strange numbness enveloped her, and Evans felt herself step back emotionally. This had nothing to do with her. Just two asshole men with an asshole father. She would help put them all in jail.

Sophie still had more to share. "The police chief was a good friend of Dennis McCarthy's and notified him of the rape victim's testimony. Then Old Man McCarthy pressured his younger son Jason, the family black sheep, to take responsibility for it." Sophie paused and took a deep breath. "I didn't have my recorder in the prison so it was a lot to keep track of. Anyway, Dennis McCarthy talked to the DA, who then rewrote the plea deal he had just offered Jason, who was out on bail. His brother Todd, on the other hand, had just started working as a deputy, so they scrubbed Todd's name from the initial report."

Jackson chimed in, his expression tight. "You're talking about Chief Owens and District Attorney Victor Slonecker?"

"Yes. This all happened right before I started at the paper, but both men were in those positions at the time."

Evans no longer cared about what had happened back then. Except for how it related to the events of two nights ago. And the reporter couldn't help them with that. "Thanks, Sophie. You're right about this being important." *Especially to Jola Shaffer.* "We have to get back to work. We'll call you if we have questions." Evans shut down the call.

The team stared at each other for a moment.

"She just accused a county law enforcement officer of

rape." Schak looked upset.

Evans swallowed hard before speaking. "What if Griffen didn't kill his ex-wife? What if Dennis McCarthy decided to clean up an old mess by silencing the one person who could cause him trouble?"

"Why now?" Schak demanded.

"Because Shaffer had been talking about the assault to her counselor. And to her sister. And her co-worker. If Shaffer was a friend of the McCarthy family, those conversations probably got back to the old man."

A heavy silence filled the room.

Jackson shifted in his chair, agitated. "There's more."

Evans turned to stare at him.

"Right before Sophie called, I glanced at Cam Le's birth certificate. The only two words I understood were *Dennis McCarthy*."

Evans glanced at the document on the table. There it was. "He's listed as her father." She felt lightheaded. "What if Cam Le heard he was running for the US presidency and contacted Dennis McCarthy?"

"Let's find out," Schak said. "We'll have to track down her phone-service provider and get her call history."

"She may have gone to meet with him in person." Evans was still reeling. "Did Dennis McCarthy kill both women to silence them and keep them from sabotaging his political aspirations?"

Jackson stood. "Let's go talk to Todd McCarthy first and see what he has to say about the old assault."

Evans got up too. "I know just where to find him."

Chapter 38

Evans' thoughts raced as she sped toward the downtown area. The studio was only five minutes away, and she had to get herself into the right frame of mind. Had she just been blind and stupid about Todd? She hadn't realized his politics until earlier today, and apparently she'd been oblivious to his true nature as well. She tried to recall things Todd might have done or said that could have given her a clue. But Evans couldn't come up with anything. That didn't surprise her. The most devastating thing the #MeToo movement had revealed was that seemingly ordinary men—and many successful ones—were capable of sexual assault and rape. And intimidation. There was no way to know who they were until their victims found the courage to share their experiences. But at least Todd wasn't the killer. Still, it appeared that his father might be, so Todd would likely not handle any of this well.

He was also a law enforcement officer who might be armed—and whose girlfriend had just broken up with him.

Her phone rang again, but Evans kept driving and ignored it. Jackson had been trying to call her, but she knew what he would say. She glanced in her rearview mirror. He was in the vehicle right behind her. Schak and Quince were trying to locate and pick up Dennis McCarthy, but that could take time. The candidate could be campaigning in another part of the state.

Evans pulled into the building's back parking lot, hoping the studio had its own entrance. She climbed out of her car and took deep breaths.

Jackson pulled in a moment later, got out, and ran toward her. "Let me take the lead on this. You're too close to it."

Evans shook her head. At the end of the meeting, she'd told the team she'd been dating Todd McCarthy, had given everyone their assignments, then bolted from the conference room before anyone could argue. She wanted to do this her way. She still wasn't quite sure what that meant—except that she intended to be non-confrontational. "I can approach Todd without setting off his internal alarms. Let me try."

Jackson grabbed her arm and squeezed. "Don't get too close to him. And if I signal you, back off. That's an order."

Evans didn't argue. She spun toward the back door and tried the handle. Locked. *Damn!* She jogged around to the front of the building with Jackson a half-step behind her. The front door was locked too. No surprise. It was after hours. But she knew Todd was still inside, recording campaign ads. His vehicle was right there. She gestured with her head. "That's his Cherokee. Should we disable it?"

"No." Jackson's expression was grim. "He might lead us straight to his father."

"Good call." Dennis McCarthy was the homicide suspect. She had to keep him as the priority. But her anger was channeled at Todd. He's the one who had fooled her. Evans pounded on the glass door.

A minute later, the same receptionist from earlier hustled into the lobby. She used an intercom to communicate. "I'm sorry, but we're closed to the public now."

Evans found the exterior panel and pressed the talk button. "I was here this afternoon, remember? I'm Todd

McCarthy's friend. He invited me to come back."

"Oh, right." The young woman unlocked the door and opened it a few inches. "Who's the guy with you?"

"Another friend of Todd's."

"I can't let him in, just you."

Jackson stepped up beside Evans and held out his badge, something he rarely did. "We're both coming inside."

The receptionist looked startled, but she pushed open the door and held it for them. "What's going on?"

"Nothing," Evans said, feeling impatient. "Is the studio unlocked?"

"Yes."

"Good. Now go home."

"But I'm not off work until—"

"Just go." Evans didn't want her coming back and interrupting.

The woman grabbed her purse and sweater from behind the desk and hurried out.

Evans started down the hall, realizing that other employees were probably in the building too. A cameraman, a sound technician, and possible more. *It would be okay,* she told herself. Todd wasn't violent, and they weren't here to arrest him. He might never be held accountable for the rape. Her end-goal objective was to learn if he and/or his father had an alibi for either of the homicides' window of opportunity. She really hoped Todd did. But she would start by asking him about Jola Shaffer and see how he reacted.

She entered the studio, held the door for Jackson, then paused in the waiting area. Evans glanced at the lockers. Would Todd have put his service weapon in there? Would he even have brought it with him here? Most law enforcement officers never went anywhere unarmed, herself included. For them, not carrying a gun was like walking around naked. Only worse. If she had to choose between clothes and a weapon, she would pick the weapon. She'd become that way on the job. Having people threaten her every day as a patrol cop had made her a little jumpy.

Jackson touched her shoulder. "Ready?"

She nodded.

"I've got your back." He patted the Sig Sauer under his jacket.

Evans pulled the heavy curtain away from the wall and slipped into the next room.

"Hey," someone whispered. "We're shooting." A tech guy with an earpiece sidled up next to her. "You need to wait outside."

"Todd invited me."

He made a small noise of complaint in his throat, then whispered, "Stay back and be quiet. We're almost done with this take."

At the other end of the dim room, Todd stood in a bright circle of light, talking to potential voters about his father. This speech was different from the one she'd heard and focused on economic issues. How many ads was he making? He'd been going strong for five hours already. They'd probably done dozens of takes for each one. The cameraman—who was likely the director too—called "Cut." Muted overhead lights came on while the spotlight on Todd faded out. He walked toward the cameraman, not seeing her.

"Hey, Todd. Do you have a minute?" Evans moved toward him, her heart rate picking up.

"Lara. You're back." Todd gave her a tight smile and started her way. He spotted Jackson and abruptly stopped. "Who's your friend?"

"Just another detective I was riding with." She smiled gently. "Can we talk?"

"I don't know. You broke up with me on a voice message. That was pretty shitty." Todd took two steps back.

Was he inching toward the rear exit?

"I know. I should have waited until I saw you. I'm sorry. I just didn't realize your politics until today." All true. Evans eased forward again, feeling Jackson move in unison behind her. She glanced around to see if Todd had a jacket or a satchel somewhere, but she couldn't tell. The lighting was weird, and too many cables and monitors were in her way. She pushed between two giant speakers, and Jackson went around them.

"But that's not what I want to ask you," she called out.

"I don't feel like talking. And I'm not done recording. So just leave."

"First, I need to learn something. Do you know Jola Shaffer?"

Todd's body stiffened and his face seemed to freeze. "No. Why?"

"Let's just say I'm a jealous ex-girlfriend. You've never met Jola?"

"Not that I know of."

Liar! There could be only one reason for him to pretend to not know Jola. Evans accepted that the stories about his sexual assault were true. She let that go for now to focus on Dennis McCarthy. "Where is your dad?"

"On his way here. We're recording a segment together. Why?"

Not ideal. They wanted to talk to the old man but not with his son present. "We need some information."

Todd reached around to his back pocket.

"Stop!" Evans and Jackson yelled at the same time.

"What the hell? I was just getting my phone."

"It can wait." Evans kept her voice soft. "Will you come into the department with me? Answer some questions?" She wanted to get Todd out before his dad showed up. They had to question them separately. Maybe pit them against each other.

"I'm in the middle of something important here. Maybe tomorrow after my shift."

"Our investigation takes priority. You're a cop; you know that."

"I'm destined for bigger things. You could have come along with me. It's your loss." A bitter smile seemed to freeze on his face.

"What's going on?" The voice came from behind them.

Evans kept her eyes on Todd, trusting Jackson to check out the newcomer. But she knew who he was. Anyone who followed politics did.

"State your name," Jackson said.

"Governor Dennis McCarthy." He spoke with authority, a man who expected to be listened to.

"Good," Jackson said. "We need to talk."

Evans glanced over at the governor. Tall, sixty-something with thinning hair, but attractive. And clearly Todd's father. They had the same nose and forehead.

Jackson moved in front of the candidate, trying to separate him from his son. "I'd like you to come into the department and answer questions."

"What is this about? I'm a busy man with people on the clock here." He used anger and bluster to sound intimidating.

"Do you know Cam Le?" Jackson asked.

"Who?" An edge of concern.

"A woman from Viet Nam who came here to find you. She has a birth certificate with your name on it."

"She sounds like a scammer." The father shot a look at his son.

They both knew about Cam Le?

"Did she contact you?" Jackson pressed.

"I don't have time for this. Just get out of here. We have a campaign to run."

The older man strode around Jackson to reach the spotlight area where his son stood. At the same time, Todd darted for a stool next to the wall. He snatched up his jacket and reached for something under it.

Evans and Jackson both drew their weapons. "Hands in the air!" Evans shouted.

Todd let the jacket fall to the floor, exposing his service weapon. He grabbed it and rushed to his father. Ducking behind him, Todd used the older man as a shield and hostage.

What was he doing? "Todd, put your gun down! We just want to question your father. We know about the rape, but that's not why we're here." Todd's actions unnerved Evans. He acted like a man with nothing to lose.

"No! You disarm!" Todd shifted and waved his gun at the cameraman. "Plug me into all the networks." Next he raised the weapon to his father's head and shouted, "All of you do as I say or you'll end up killing a presidential candidate on live TV!"

Jackson bellowed at the studio people, "Get out! Now!"

Keeping his father in front, Todd sidestepped toward the cameraman and threatened, "Connect me!"

"I'll get fired."

"Not a chance. Audiences will love this."

Holy shit! This was a PR stunt. At the expense of real

murder investigations.

The studio tech stepped over to a panel of switches and clicked several. "Going live in five seconds."

Todd raised his weapon and pointed it straight at Evans, who was closest to him. "Get back!"

"This is foolish," she called. "You're outmanned! And more officers are coming."

"If I have to talk about this, I want the public to hear it straight from me." Todd turned to the shaking cameraman and barked, "Bring the lens in closer."

Evans glanced at Jackson, who mouthed, *Let him talk.*

Todd stared straight into the camera as a soft countdown timer pinged, indicating a live broadcast. "This is Deputy Todd McCarthy. I'm here with my father, presidential candidate Dennis McCarthy."

Chapter 39

A few minutes earlier

Relieved that her intense round-trip drive was over, Sophie took the first Eugene exit. With her earpiece still in place, she called Dennis McCarthy's office again. A staffer finally answered. "Dennis McCarthy for President campaign headquarters. This is Tanya."

"Sophie Speranza, *Willamette News*. I really need to talk to Governor McCarthy. This involves his son and some serious allegations against the candidate." Sophie tried to sound earnest. "I want to give Mr. McCarthy a chance to respond before I go to press with them."

"What allegations?" The young woman was rightly worried.

"You're wasting precious time. Just get him on the phone, wherever he is, and tell him he needs to meet with me right now." Sophie slowed for the down ramp, unsure of which direction to turn. "If not, McCarthy will see the story in the paper tomorrow morning without his comments. Do you need my number?"

"No, I have it. You've left a few messages." A silence while the staffer made a decision. "Mr. McCarthy is at the new Vortex studio right now to record a campaign ad. I'm sure he'd be happy to give you a statement."

He wouldn't be happy about it, but he would have something to say.

"Do you know where it is?" the woman asked.

"Yes." She'd been there a few times. "Thanks." Sophie pressed her earpiece, hoping she hadn't been lied to. She really did want to hear what McCarthy would say about the allegations and include his response in her profile piece. Good journalism required it. She also wanted to question the police chief and the DA who'd been involved in the cover-up. But Chief Owens would never speak to her, and Victor Slonecker was dead. But his amorality was a known fact, so she didn't doubt his role in the incident. He'd probably been well paid.

Sophie turned left toward the downtown studio, eager to confront McCarthy—about everything.

Chapter 40

Stunned by Todd's bold move, Jackson wasn't sure how to handle the situation. Neither training nor experience covered it. He and Evans would have to wing it, with the first objective to keep everyone alive. Then hope like hell they didn't freak out the public with a live broadcast. But which of these men was their suspect? Todd was acting like a guilty man, but maybe he was taking the hit for his dad, trying to turn this confrontation into a reality show and popularity boost. Or maybe the two had colluded to silence both women—and were still working together.

Todd, using a *serious-actor* tone undercut by jitters, communicated to a live primetime audience. "First, let me say that this man is the finest person to ever run for the office of president. And his first priority is to restore the rule of law. Real law. Not this politically correct bullshit we see in liberal towns like Eugene and sanctuary cities like San Francisco."

What the hell was he talking about? Jackson stepped toward Todd. "Put the gun down! There's no way out of this." That would be true if the SWAT unit was actually on the way with a dozen men, including snipers who could take out Todd without harming anyone else. But nobody had reported the incident. Could he make an SOS call without getting shot? He didn't believe Todd would hurt his own father, but the bastard might kill him.

"In fact, I'm in this position right now," Todd informed viewers, "because local law enforcement has wrongly accused my father. Don't believe a word of it! They're just trying to smear him because they don't like his politics and want him to drop out of the race. He's innocent! We're both innocent."

"Innocent of what?" Jackson hollered. "The murder of Cam Le? His own daughter who he fathered in Viet Nam?"

"A lie and a scam!" Todd yelled back. "Those people will do anything for money."

"What about Jola Shaffer? The woman you—"

Todd shouted over him. "Shut up! I'm calling the shots here." He stepped backward toward the exit, pulling his dad with him.

The older man, who had seemed too stunned to speak, finally mumbled, "Todd, let's find a better way. I can withdraw from the race."

"No! This is the only way to save your candidacy." He projected his voice toward the camera. "If they shoot this man, it will be for political reasons. They're afraid he'll win, and the liberal left will do anything to take him down!"

Crazy and clever. But if Todd McCarthy thought he could hamstring a police operation with this bullshit, he was wrong. As a deputy, he should know better. "No one has to get shot today!" Jackson bellowed back. "Put your weapon down and let go of the hostage!"

But Todd was still backing toward the exit, taking his dad. Jackson, Evans, and the cameraman all moved in unison with him.

"Wait!" A shrill voice was suddenly in the room.

Jackson glanced sideways to see Sophie Speranza running into the line of the camera.

"Get back!" he shouted.

"I have more information," she said, ignoring his order. "And everyone needs to hear it."

Chapter 41

Oh shit! Sophie froze. Todd McCarthy had a gun. And it was held to his own father's head. What the hell was going on? She glanced around and spotted the red lights on the camera. And the guns drawn. She hadn't seen the weapons until she'd passed the detectives. No wonder Jackson had yelled at her. But it was too late to back off now. If the camera was running, then Todd McCarthy wanted media attention. She would give him a little more. "I'm a reporter," she said softly. "I can help tell your side of this."

"The whole country is watching," the younger man said. "We don't need you. Get out before you get hurt."

It wasn't a direct threat. And he couldn't shoot at her without stepping from behind his human shield. Sophie locked eyes on Dennis McCarthy. "I know about what happened in Viet Nam. A fellow soldier told me he witnessed you kill your commander." She eventually wanted him to talk about covering up his older son's rape, but instinct told her this subject would trigger him. And the truth would come out with his emotions. She pressed on. "I understand why you did it. You wanted to stop the killing."

Dennis blinked and stared without seeing her.

"You'd been following orders," she prompted, "but you just couldn't do it anymore."

Something inside the older man seemed to break. His shoulders slumped, and his head dropped in shame.

"This is your chance to help everyone understand," Sophie pleaded softly. "A lot of Americans still don't know what it was like over there."

"It was hell on earth!" The anguish in Dennis's voice matched the expression on his face.

"Why? What were your orders?"

"To kill every gook we encountered in the fields. And they were all women and children." His voice broke. "And I just couldn't do it anymore. The whole unit tried protesting. We went out and just sat down in the jungle all day. Didn't shoot anyone. But the commander beat the hell out of Brantley and made us watch. Told us there would be more if we didn't kill the damn enemy as ordered." Tears rolled down his face as he shared his memories. "But the farmers, the women and children, they were just living their lives. Growing rice and singing as they worked. We shot kids who were singing!"

Dennis McCarthy sobbed for a moment. When he had control, Sophie prodded him again. "So you killed your commander? To stop him from giving you orders?"

"Yes! I knifed him in the back with a farming tool I took off a dead Viet girl. Three days later, they put us all on a plane home. I don't know if it was Brantley who told you this part, but I saved his life. He was going to kill himself rather than shoot one more woman." McCarthy shuddered. "A lot of soldiers did commit suicide. Others took heroin to numb themselves. The whole war was fucked up beyond all recognition."

"I'm sorry for your pain," Sophie said, glancing back at the detectives. Their guns were still drawn, but they weren't signaling her to stop. Getting a hostage-taker to talk was a police tactic. She had just used it on the hostage instead. And she couldn't really see Todd.

McCarthy seemed old and beaten, but she couldn't let him off the hook. Sophie sucked in a breath and blurted it out. "I just talked to your son Jason at Deer Ridge. He had a lot to say about the rape charge he's doing time for."

"Shut up!" Todd bellowed from behind his father. He tugged on the older man. "We're getting out of here."

"Not yet," Dennis countered, resisting his son. "This all has to come out. I know you tried to help bury anything that could hurt my campaign, but the police seem to know."

Todd McCarthy had killed Jola Shaffer? Sophie struggled to stay low-key. "Yes, we all know Todd committed the assault on Jola Shaffer." Sophie eased to the right, half-expecting Jackson to charge at the men. But he didn't, so she pressed for more—jealous that the networks were getting all this live. "Was it your idea to shift blame to your younger son Jason?"

"It doesn't matter. We all collaborated to pull it off." Dennis let out a bitter laugh. "A politician can survive having one son in prison, but not two."

"Dad, just shut up!" Todd's voice quivered. He knew he'd lost control of the situation. And his cover-up.

The older man turned to face his son. "I'm proud of you and your career in law enforcement. You more than made up for your mistake."

Sophie stiffened. Rape was an assault—one that often ruined the victim's mental health. Calling it a *mistake* was revolting. Thank goodness this asshole was no longer headed for the presidency. She started to ask Todd a question, but he cut her off.

"Those cunts just wanted to sabotage my dad's campaign. They're political operatives who got paid! That Asian bitch actually tried to extort money out of me."

Paranoid, misogynistic, and losing it! As a woman who was exposing the truth, Sophie was suddenly worried for her safety. She took another step away.

"That's right, get back! All of you! Or I'll shoot the reporter!"

Chapter 42

Jackson braced for the worst. But no shots rang out. Nor did he have a clear one to take. Not without hitting the hostage. But Dennis McCarthy was a criminal too and probably not in any real danger from his son. Jackson reassessed that. Todd could suddenly kill his father and himself. They were both men with nothing left to lose. But they had to be stopped before they took anyone with them. And Sophie was still in the line of fire.

"Drop the weapon!" he shouted again. "Let this end with no more deaths!"

The father and son both lunged backward out the door, then slammed it shut. Jackson bolted after them.

By the time he reached the exterior parking lot, the two men were climbing into Todd's vehicle. With his weapon still aimed at Todd, who was driving, Jackson reached for his phone with his free hand and pressed 911.

He cut into the dispatcher's greeting. "Jackson here. We have a hostage situation. White Cherokee jeep. Bravo, Echo, Oscar, eight, five, zero. Two men. The driver is armed and dangerous."

The engine roared and Todd lurched toward the exit.

"Should I take out a tire?" Evans asked, shouting over the noise.

"If you can." Jackson still had the damn phone to his ear, trying to hear what the dispatcher was asking.

"Where is your location?"

"Sixth and Pearl."

"Shit!" Evans yelled in his other ear.

A cyclist was riding across the sidewalk behind the jeep, right into her line of fire.

"Move!" she shouted, running toward the vehicle.

The cyclist stopped and stared—then noticed the guns and quickly moved on.

But the white jeep had sped away.

"Shit!" Evans bolted for her car.

Jackson did the same, shouting "Road blocks!" at the dispatcher. The McCarthys wouldn't get far.

Chapter 43

Todd McCarthy's heart pounded so hard he thought it would burst from his chest. He'd been involved in some tense law-enforcement operations before—but never like this. He could have pulled off the whole thing if his father had kept his mouth shut. "Why, Dad? Why talk about goddamn Viet Nam?"

"The story was out." His father sounded frustrated, but old and tired too. "Brantley finally told somebody. A reporter! Forty-some years later."

Todd headed for the I-5 on-ramp. "You should have denied it! Nobody cares about Viet Nam anymore. And the base loves you." Impulsively, he punched his dad in the arm. "Goddamnit! I had you covered. Casting doubt on the detectives' motive would have worked. I would have beat the stupid murder charges. *If* they had even charged me. They've got nothing."

"Not anymore."

No shit! His dad had fucked this up so badly. Todd didn't know what to do next. All he was certain about was that he couldn't go to prison. He couldn't even make himself visit his brother. Just hearing the doors shut behind him made him crazy.

His dad hit him back. "You did this! Taking a hostage in front of cops is not a charge you can ever beat."

"My own father? They knew you were never at risk. A jury would end up split on the issue." His frustration threatened to consume him. Todd pressed the gas and shot up the ramp onto the freeway. "The media coverage would have boosted your poll numbers and won you the nomination! Yeah, I would have lost my job, but who cares? You were gonna give me a better one in DC."

Heart still hammering like a locomotive, Todd glanced into the rearview mirror. No black sedans or blue SUVS after him yet.

"You didn't have to kill those women." His dad punched his arm again. "You could have just taken the damn birth certificate and destroyed it. Without the document, her story was old news." The older man shook his head. "And Jola was a drunk whore. The police barely took her seriously. I just offered—"

"Shut up about Jola." Todd had loved her once . . . long ago. But her reporting their quickie as a rape had been vindictive. He'd never forgiven her. Still, he'd been relieved to find her passed out. Holding the pillow over her face hadn't been that painful for either of them. The little Asian woman was a money-grubbing blackmailer and completely disposable. He hadn't given her a second thought.

His father suddenly grabbed his arm and pleaded, "Just pull over and end this. We'll hire the best lawyers we can. We'll call the murders a political hit. A frame job!"

Todd jerked his arm free, swerving to miss another car. "Too late! You already admitted to covering up the rape charge. You can't overcome that." Todd slammed his hand into the wheel. "But you're right about Jola. Her story was bullshit even back then. She never said no."

"I always believed you."

"I wish you'd believed in me a moment ago and kept it together."

"I'm sorry, son. I had a bad moment. The Nam memories got to me."

The blare of sirens filled the air, rattling Todd's frayed nerves. "I guess we're not running to Canada."

His dad suddenly laughed, a strange half-amused, half-tortured sound. "It might be fun to try."

Could they? As a county deputy, he knew the back roads better than anyone. He would get off the freeway in Springfield and head north from there. He strained to see ahead, calculating how long it would take to reach the exit. A few more seconds.

The sirens grew louder.

Todd glanced into the rearview mirror. Directly behind him was a family car, but beyond that, a dark sedan was gaining on him. Behind it, red and blue lights flashed. He pressed the accelerator to the floor and screamed around the truck in front. A second later, he cut back into the right lane—just in time to take the Glenwood exit. He prayed for the driver behind him to exit as well. The cop in the sedan might not even see his vehicle on the exit ramp.

But he needed more distance. Todd kept his foot to the floor. A stop sign appeared at the bottom of the long ramp. *Oh hell!* Time to slow down or he'd run the intersection.

He braked but couldn't get the jeep's momentum under control. They blew past the stop sign.

A frantic driver pulled into the median to avoid getting plowed. A business loomed ahead. A restaurant full of people. Todd pressed the brake harder. The pedal went to the floor, and they started to slow down.

"Watch out!" his father shouted.

Oh shit! An old gas station beyond the restaurant had just come into view. Todd pulled to the left, hoping to stay on the road. But it was too late. They plowed into it, hitting a pump dead on. First the airbag slammed into his chest, a crushing pain. A split-second later, the roar of the explosion deafened him. Then Todd closed his eyes for the last time.

Chapter 44

Friday, July 12, 9:55 a.m.

Jackson resisted a second cup of coffee, thinking a sedative was more in order. He had a press conference scheduled in a few minutes. He read through his notes again. So many details! He usually couldn't share specific information with the public because they needed it to investigate or prosecute the suspect. But for both murders, the perp was dead, and he had no good reason to hold back. Besides, much of the public had already witnessed the McCarthy men's staged hostage scenario and half-assed confession.

Evans stuck her head into his cube. "Ready?"

Jackson stood, braced himself, and trotted downstairs with Evans and Schak following. A patrol officer waiting in the lobby opened the door, then followed them out. His uniformed presence was meant to deter anyone from coming up and getting too close. Lammers wanted the other detectives present as a show of manpower and united thinking.

Jackson stopped at the edge of the wide landing and stood in front of the microphone. At the base of the short flight of steps, a crowd of reporters and onlookers waited. TV cameras, small handhelds, microphones, cables, and a few yellow tablets. Jackson spotted Sophie in front, smiling at him like they were old friends. Her presence unexpectedly took some edge off his anxiety. He pulled in a deep breath and launched into his remarks.

"Thank you for coming. I'm Detective Jackson with the Violent Crimes Unit of the Eugene Police Department." He smiled. "For those of you who want to know my full credentials."

A few people laughed.

"This past week has been one of the most violent and disturbing our town has experienced. But I want to assure citizens that the police department is ready and able to respond to all threats." Lammers had given him that statement to open with, but he was onboard. Jackson continued. "First, I'll address the incendiary devices found here on police property. They have been thoroughly examined by experts and were, in fact, potentially flammable. In common terms, they're called Molotov cocktails and can generate a small explosion when smashed against a hard surface. But these were left sitting, inactivated. We think the perpetrator was sending a message. But we are not intimidated and have increased our security around the building."

"How many devices?" Sophie called out.

"Four."

"And who left them?"

He gave her a tight smile. "I'm getting to that." The day was already warm, and he wished he could take off his jacket. "The devices placed here on our property were similar to the incendiaries used to start the fire at the Golden Temple restaurant two nights ago. More such devices were found at the Lucky Noodle, another nearby restaurant. We searched the suspect's home and found even more of the same materials. We believe the same person is responsible for all these crimes."

"Wasn't he shot?" A young TV reporter shouted this time.

"Yes. Buck Hinsic, the leader of a white nationalist group called the Homelanders, was shot and killed by the restaurant's owner. The owner had been assaulted a week earlier, and we believe Hinsic committed that crime as well." Jackson hoped to keep Pham's name quiet.

But no such luck.

"Who's the owner?" the same TV reporter asked.

"Mr. Pham. If you want to know more, go eat at his restaurant and ask him." Jackson smiled, even knowing Lammers would give him shit for that endorsement. Too bad. The old man needed something positive to come out of this.

"What was Hinsic's motive?" Sophie asked.

She already knew, so he guessed she wanted the facts made public. "These were all hate crimes. The Homelanders, whose main organization is in Portland, are known to target Hispanic- and Asian-owned businesses. We know who the local members are, and we will be watching them closely." Jackson felt sweat on his forehead so he paused to unbutton his jacket and mentally shift gears.

"Did he kill the Asian woman whose photo we shared on the news?" A middle-aged guy with a cameraman nearby asked the question for him.

"No. Her name is Cam Le, and her death is more complicated. Most of the details surrounding the incident played out on live TV last night."

"Give us a recap," an older woman in the back demanded. "Not all of us watch TV."

Jackson dreaded this part and hoped to get through it quickly. He hated bringing politics into police work, but except for crimes of passion, sociopolitical issues motivated most criminal acts. "We've concluded that Cam Le was murdered by Todd McCarthy, a deputy with the Lane County Sheriff's Department. His motive for killing her was rooted in ambition. Based on a birth certificate she carried, we believe she was his half-sister. Cam Le had traveled to our country to confront her father, Governor Dennis McCarthy, who had become a presidential candidate. We're still waiting on the DNA tests to confirm their biological connections, but Dennis McCarthy had an opportunity to deny his parentage, and he didn't."

"You're saying Todd McCarthy killed her to silence her?" the middle-aged TV reporter asked. "To protect his father's candidacy?"

"We believe so."

"That seems extreme," he commented. "A lot of veterans fathered children with Viet women."

Jackson didn't know what to say.

But Sophie did. She turned to the newscaster and spoke into his microphone. "I interviewed a Viet Nam vet who served next to Dennis McCarthy, and he says McCarthy raped Viet women. So Cam Le's conception may have been a crime too."

Reporters started shouting questions, some at Sophie and some at Jackson, while the citizens whispered amongst themselves. When the chaos died down, Jackson tried to get through the rest of his talking points. "We also found a letter in Cam Le's personal papers. It was written by her mother and confirms that she was raped by Dennis McCarthy."

"What a piece of shit!" the older woman in back shouted.

Jackson concurred but tried to remain expressionless. His next announcement would be a bombshell. "Another sexual assault took place eight years ago. The victim, Jola Shaffer, was murdered Monday night, twenty-four hours after Cam Le was killed. The perpetrator was the same man, Todd McCarthy. He silenced Jola Shaffer to cover his own criminal behavior and indirectly benefit his father's campaign."

A few of the citizens in the crowd gasped.

Jackson had one more news-bomb for those who didn't watch TV. "Both Todd and Dennis McCarthy died in an accident as they fled from police."

A moment of quiet, then Sophie shouted, "Tell us about the cover-up!"

Jackson had hoped to avoid that. Sophie was now back on his shit list. "This is a new investigation for us, and it's still in the preliminary stages. All we know is that witnesses claim the wrong man was sentenced to prison for Jola Shaffer's rape and that high-ranking officials, including Dennis McCarthy, arranged for that deception and injustice."

"Who is the wrong man?" Sophie asked, pressing him to release details again.

"Jason McCarthy, the perp's brother." Jackson decided to shut down the exchange. The TV reporters would just give a brief overview of the crimes anyway, and Sophie, the only print journalist, already had the information. "That's all I have for now. Thank you for your time." He turned and started to walk away.

But Sophie called after him. "Will Chief Owen retire now that his part in the cover-up has been exposed?"

Jackson ignored her and kept moving. He wasn't authorized to talk about internal department issues. But he had a different one on his mind. When the three of them reached their workspace upstairs, he stopped and turned to his teammates. "I have an issue to deal with and I'd like your input."

"What now?" Schak asked.

"It's Jasmine Parker. I think she's dating Sophie and giving her forensic information about ongoing cases."

"What the hell?" Schak made a face. "Why do you think they're gay?"

"I don't care about their sexuality." Jackson wasn't even sure about that part. But he explained what he'd seen on his accidental FaceTime call to Sophie.

"Oh, then they're dating," Evans said. "And I don't care about that part either. But now we know how Sophie seems to have details we haven't released."

"What should I do about it?" Jackson hated the thought of Parker being fired. "It's a serious breach of trust. I can't just let it go."

"So talk to her," Evans suggested. "Tell Parker you know and that she has to stop. I'm sure she will."

"I don't know," Schak countered. "Maybe you should report it to Lammers."

Damn. Jackson had hoped to get a consensus. "I thought that at first too. But looking back, I'm pretty sure everything Parker shared with Sophie soon became public anyway. Our cases were never compromised. In fact, Sophie's input has helped us repeatedly." He hated admitting it, but that didn't change the fact.

"Okay," Schak said. "Just give Parker a warning."

Relieved, Jackson decided to have the difficult conversation that afternoon and be done with it. He hoped for Parker's sake that she would eventually feel free to be open about her sexuality—just not their case details. "Now let's get this meeting over with."

Chapter 45

Evans followed Jackson into the conference room, where Quince was already waiting. The team still had a few wrap-up details to discuss—mostly for their own sense of closure.

"How did it go?" Quince asked.

"Not bad." Jackson sat at the end of the table as usual. "But dear Sophie, with her inside information, kept asking loaded questions."

Evans felt a debt of gratitude for the obsessive reporter—even though it had been painful to hear the truth about Todd. "She came through for us again," Evans argued. "We would never have made the Shaffer-McCarthy connection without Sophie's trip to the prison."

"We might have." Quince grinned. "While you guys were out chatting with the press, Sprint came through with Shaffer's phone records. So I've been scanning them. Guess what?"

No one wanted to play. But Evans knew what he would say.

"Shaffer called Todd McCarthy a week before her death. I only know that because I was specifically looking for his number."

That left no doubt in her mind. Todd had suffocated the depressed woman. Evans tried to keep her face stoic. Part of her had held onto the idea that the killer could have been his father. That Dennis McCarthy had more to lose by the old rape/cover-up revelation than Todd did. But she had to let it all go. She'd gotten good at that. "Shaffer probably threatened to go public with her story, particularly about Dennis McCarthy's role in the whole thing."

"That seems likely," Jackson said. "McCarthy should have given more thought to his past crimes before he announced his run for the presidency. Apparently the women he'd wronged couldn't stand the thought of him becoming the most powerful man on the planet."

The significance of that possibility left them all silent for a moment. Finally, Evans asked, "What about Owens? Has anyone confronted the chief?"

Jackson shook his head, looking relieved. "The other detective team has finished their testimony in court, so Lammers assigned them to investigate the allegations that Owens and Slonecker arranged for the wrong man to serve prison time."

Schak made an exaggerated wiping gesture across his forehead. "Whew! I want no part of that one. I'm still hoping to collect a pension."

They all laughed. But Evans had mixed feelings. "I know Owens and Dennis McCarthy are friends, but that doesn't mean the chief knew Todd was guilty. Maybe McCarthy lied and told him Jason had committed the rape and he just needed help getting Todd's name out of the original report."

"I'd like to think that too." Jackson didn't look convinced. "We may never know."

Schak snorted. "I have no faith in leadership of any kind anymore."

Quince gave his shoulder a stiff push. "Don't be so cynical. Our experiences with criminals don't represent the larger world."

Jackson shook his head. "I don't know about that. Hate crimes are on the rise everywhere."

Evans was still coming to terms with the fact that a man she'd been intimate with had committed two murders. She wondered how many other men in the world were like that. Seeming fairly normal on the surface, yet capable of evil. She shuddered.

Jackson reached over and squeezed her shoulder. "Hey, if you need some time off, take it. I'll talk to Lammers."

Evans smiled at him. "I'm fine." She looked over at Schak and Quince. "But you guys have to cut me some slack if I ever date again. No teasing me about running the guy's profile in the serial-killer database."

They both laughed. But Schak got the last word. "No problem. As long as you let me chaperone your first three dates."

Evans laughed too. "Deal." These three were good men, and she had to believe that there were a lot more like them out there.

Chapter 46

Jackson pulled down the long panhandle driveway and rounded the corner. The property opened into a half-acre park-like setting with a big house in the back. He loved it already. The boys could climb trees and play soccer right in their own yard. He turned to Kera. "It's perfect. I don't even need to see the inside."

She smiled. "That's how I felt when I saw it too. But I checked out the interior anyway. And it's lovely."

Jackson parked in front of the garage, then helped the boys out of their car seats. They scrambled to get free and run toward the rope swing. Jackson smiled at their joy.

Kera soon called them back. "Let's check out the inside again."

She unlocked the door, and they wandered through the living room and family room. He loved the extra space and bright daylight from the large windows. "This would be a great house to buy," he mused.

"I think so too. And when our yearlong lease is up, we have that option. The owners will apply all of our rent to the down payment."

"Sounds like we'll be buying a house a year from now." Jackson grinned at Kera. "If everything goes according to plan."

She laughed. "It will be a first for us if it does." She gestured for him to follow. "Come see the master bedroom."

They looked at the other bedrooms as well. In the last one, Kera said, "The boys can share a room for now, and we'll set up this one as our office."

Jackson nodded. "You mean 'share a room' until Katie moves out." His daughter was working a lunch shift at her new job.

"You know it's coming." Kera rubbed his arm. "But we'll find ways to keep her close."

Overwhelmed with emotions, Jackson couldn't speak. He let go of his sadness about Katie's impending departure and embraced the joy of his new family. Life was constantly changing, and he'd learned to roll with it.

The boys ran out of the room, eager to see the garage. On impulse, Jackson pulled Kera in for a tight hug and whispered, "Marry me."

She kissed him passionately and whispered back, "I'll think about it."

L.J. Sellers writes the bestselling Detective Jackson mysteries—a five-time Readers Favorite Award winner. She also pens the high-octane Agent Dallas series, the new Extractor series, and provocative standalone thrillers. Her 25 novels have been highly praised by reviewers, and she's one of the highest-rated crime fiction authors on Amazon.

Detective Jackson Mysteries:

The Sex Club
Secrets to Die For
Thrilled to Death
Passions of the Dead
Dying for Justice
Liars, Cheaters & Thieves
Rules of Crime
Crimes of Memory
Deadly Bonds
Wrongful Death
Death Deserved
A Bitter Dying
A Liar's Death
A Crime of Hate

Agent Dallas Thrillers:

The Trigger
The Target
The Trap

Standalone Thrillers:
Guilt Game
The Gender Experiment
Point of Control
The Baby Thief
The Gauntlet Assassin
The Lethal Effect

L.J. resides in Eugene, Oregon where many of her novels are set and is an award-winning journalist who earned the Grand Neal. When not plotting murders, she enjoys standup comedy, cycling, and zip-lining. She's also been known to jump out of airplanes..

Thanks for reading my novel. If you enjoyed it, please leave a review or rating online. Find out more about my work at ljsellers.com, where you can sign up to hear about new releases. —L.J.